THE TEETH OF DEATH

It was uncanny to hear the words issuing from the mouth of an ape—one of Pew Mogel's monstrous guards, endowed with a human brain.

John Carter, Dejah Thoris and Tars Tarkas, imprisoned in the cage, watched the surface of the water come nearer as it was lowered. Then the three captives saw the slanting, evil eyes, the rows of flashing teeth in a dozen hideous reptilian jaws staring up at them.

"Quite ingenious," remarked Tars Tarkas with sardonic grimness.

John Carter's eyes were fastened on the bank of the pit. He could just see one of the sleeping ape-guard's feet. If he could manage to set the cage swinging enough . . .

Edgar Rice Burroughs
MARS NOVELS
Now available from Ballantine Books:

A PRINCESS OF MARS (#1)
THE GODS OF MARS (#2)
THE WARLORD OF MARS (#3)
THUVIA, MAID OF MARS (#4)
THE CHESSMEN OF MARS (#5)
THE MASTER MIND OF MARS (#6)
A FIGHTING MAN OF MARS (#7)
SWORDS OF MARS (#8)
SYNTHETIC MEN OF MARS (#9)
LLANA OF GATHOL (#10)
JOHN CARTER OF MARS (#11)

JOHN CARTER OF MARS

Edgar Rice Burroughs

BALLANTINE BOOKS • NEW YORK

John Carter of Mars was first published in two parts
in *Amazing Stories Magazine* as follows:
Part 1. "John Carter and the Giant of Mars," January, 1941
         Copyright © 1940 Ziff-Davis Publishing Company
Part 2. "Skeleton Men of Jupiter," February, 1943
         Copyright © 1942 Ziff-Davis Publishing Company

Library of Congress Catalog Card Number: 64-15790

ISBN 0-345-27844-5

This authorized edition published by arrangement
with Edgar Rice Burroughs, Inc.

Manufactured in the United States of America

First U.S. Printing: April 1965
Ninth U.S. Printing: April 1979

First Canadian Printing: June 1965
Third Canadian Printing: April 1979

Cover art by Michael Whelan, Copyright © 1979
Edgar Rice Burroughs, Inc.

TABLE OF CONTENTS

JOHN CARTER
AND THE
GIANT OF MARS

ONE

Abduction

THE MOONS OF MARS looked down upon a giant Martian thoat as it raced silently over the soft mossy ground. Eight powerful legs carried the creature forward in great, leaping strides.

The path of the mighty beast was guided telepathically by the two people who sat in a huge saddle that was cinched to the thoat's broad back.

It was the custom of Dejah Thoris, Princess of Helium, to ride forth weekly to inspect part of her grandfather's vast farming and industrial kingdom.

Her journey to the farm lands wound through the lonely Helium Forest where grow the huge trees that furnish much of the lumber supply to the civilized nations of Mars.

Dawn was just breaking in the eastern Martian sky, and the jungle was dark and still damp with the evening dew. The gloom of the forest made Dejah Thoris thankful for the presence of her companion, who rode in the saddle in front of her. Her hands rested on his broad, bronze shoulders, and the feel of those smooth, supple muscles gave her a little thrill of confidence. One of his hands rested on the jewel-encrusted hilt of his great long sword; and he sat his saddle very straight, for he was the mightiest warrior on Mars.

John Carter turned to gaze at the lovely face of his princess.

"Frightened, Dejah Thoris?" he asked.

"Never, when I am with my chieftain," Dejah Thoris smiled.

"But what of the forest monsters, the arboks?"

"Grandfather has had them all removed. On the last trip, my guard killed the only tree reptile I've ever seen."

Suddenly Dejah Thoris gasped, clutched vainly at John Carter to regain her balance. The mighty thoat lurched heavily to the mossy ground. The riders catapulted over his head. In an instant the two had regained their feet; but the thoat lay very still.

Carter jerked his long sword from its scabbard and motioned Dejah Thoris to stay at his back.

The silence of the forest was abruptly shattered by an uncanny roar directly above them.

"An arbok!" Dejah Thoris cried.

The tree reptile launched itself straight for the hated man-things. Carter lifted his sword and swung quickly to one side, drawing the monster's attention away from Dejah Thoris who crouched behind the fallen thoat.

The earthman's first thrust sliced harmlessly through the beast's outer skin. A huge claw knocked him off balance, and he found himself lying on the ground with the great fangs at his throat.

"Dejah Thoris, get the atom gun from the thoat's back." Carter called hoarsely to the girl. There was no answer.

Calling upon every ounce of his great strength, Carter drove his sword into the arbok's neck. The creature shuddered. A stream of blood gushed from the wound. The man wriggled from under the dead body and sprang to his feet.

"Dejah Thoris! Dejah Thoris!"

Wildly Carter searched the ground and trees surrounding the dead thoat and arbok. There was no sign of Dejah Thoris. She had utterly vanished.

A shaft of light from the rising sun filtering through the foliage glistened on an object at the earthman's feet. Carter picked up a large shell, a shell recently ejected from a silent atom gun.

Springing to the dead thoat, he examined the saddle trappings. The atom gun that he had told Dejah Thoris to fire was still in its leather boot!

The earthman stooped beside the dead thoat's head. There was a tiny, bloody hole through its skull. That shot and the charging arbok had been part of a well conceived plan to abduct Dejah Thoris, and kill him!

But Dejah Thoris—how had she disappeared so quickly, so completely?

Grimly, Carter set off at a run back to the forest toward Helium.

Noon found the earthman in a private audience-chamber of Tardos Mors, Jeddak of Helium, grandfather of Dejah Thoris.

The old jeddak was worried. He thrust a rough piece of parchment into John Carter's hand. Crude, bold letters were inscribed upon the parchment; and as Carter scanned the note his eyes burned with anger: It read:

"I, Pew Mogel, the most powerful ruler on Mars, have decided to take over the iron works of Helium. The iron will furnish me with all the ships I need to protect Helium and the other cities of Barsoom from

*invasion. If you have not evacuated all your workers
from the iron mines and factories in three days, then I
will start sending you the fingers of the Royal Princess
of Helium. Hurry, because I may decide to send her
tongue, which wags too much of John Carter. Remember, obey Pew Mogel, for he is all-powerful."*

Tardos Mors dug his nails into the palms of his
hands.

"Who is this upstart who calls himself the most
powerful ruler of Mars?"

Carter looked thoughtfully at the note.

"He must have spies here," he said. "Pew Mogel
knew that I was to leave this morning with Dejah
Thoris on a tour of inspection."

"A spy it must have been," Tardos Mors groaned.
"I found this note pinned to the curtains in my private
audience-chamber. But what can we do? Dejah Thoris
is the only thing in life that I have left to love—" His
voice broke.

"All Helium loves her, Tardos Mors, and we will
all die before we return to you empty-handed."

Carter strode to the visiscreen and pushed a button.

"Summon Kantos Kan and Tars Tarkas." He spoke
quickly to an orderly. "Have them come here at once."

Soon after, the huge, green warrior and the lean, red
man were in the audience-chamber.

"It is fortunate, John Carter, that I am here in
Helium on my weekly visit from the plains." Tars
Tarkas, the green thark, gripped his massive sword
with his powerful four hands. His great, giant body
loomed majestically above the others in the room.

Kantos Kan laid his hand on John Carter's shoulder.

"I was on my way to the palace when I received
your summons. Already, word of our princess' abduction has spread over Helium. I came immediately," said
the noble fellow, "to offer you my sword and my
heart."

"I have never heard of this Pew Mogel," said Tars Tarkas. "Is he a green man?"

Tardos Mors grunted, "He's probably some petty outlaw or criminal who has an overbloated ego."

Carter raised his eyes from the ransom note.

"No, Tardos Mors. I think he is more formidable than you imagine. He is clever, also. There must have been an airship, with a silent motor, at hand to carry Dejah Thoris away so quickly—or perhaps some great bird! Only a very powerful man who is prepared to back up his threats would kidnap the Princess of Helium and even hope to take over the great iron works.

"He probably has great resources at his command. It is doubtful, however, if he has any intention of returning the princess or he would have included more details in his ransom note."

Suddenly the earthman's keen eyes narrowed. A shadow had moved in the adjoining room.

With a powerful leap, Carter reached the arched doorway. A furtive figure melted away into the semi-gloom of the passageway, with Carter close behind.

Seeing escape impossible, the stranger halted, sank to one knee and leveled a ray-gun at the approaching figure of the earthman. Carter saw his finger whiten as he squeezed the trigger.

"Carter!" Kantos Kan shouted, "throw yourself to the floor."

With the speed of light, Carter dropped prone. A long blade whizzed over his head and buried itself to the hilt in the heart of the stranger.

"One of Pew Mogel's spies," John Carter muttered as he rose to his feet. "Thank you, Kantos Kan."

Kantos Kan searched the body but found no clue to the man's identity.

Back in the audience-chamber, the men set to work with fierce resolve.

They were bending over a huge map of Barsoom when Carter spoke.

"Cities for miles around Helium are now all friendly. They would have warned us of this Pew Mogel if they had known of him. He has probably taken over one of the deserted cities in the dead sea bottom east or west of Helium. It means thousands of miles to search; but we will go over each mile."

Carter seated himself at a table and explained his plan.

"Tars Tarkas, go east and contact the chiefs of all your tribes. I'll cover the west with air scouts. Kantos Kan will stay in Helium as contact man. Be ready night and day with the entire Helium air force. Whoever discovers Dejah Thoris first will notify Kantos Kan of his position. Naturally, we can only communicate to each other through Kantos Kan. The wave length will be constant and secret, 2000 kilocycles."

Tardos Mors turned to the earthman.

"Every resource in my kingdom is at your command, John Carter."

"We leave at once, your majesty; and if Dejah Thoris is alive on Barsoom, we shall find her," replied John Carter.

TWO

The Search

WITHIN THREE HOURS, John Carter was standing on the roof of the Royal Airdrome giving last-minute instructions to a fleet of twenty-four fast, one-man scouts.

"Cover all the territory in your district thoroughly. If you discover anything, don't attempt to handle it by yourself. Notify Kantos Kan immediately." Carter surveyed the grim faces before him and knew that they would obey him.

"Let's go." Carter jerked a thumb over his shoulder to the ships.

The men scattered and soon their planes were speeding away from Helium.

Carter stayed on the roof long enough to check with Kantos Kan. He adjusted the earphones around his head and then signalled on 2000 kilocycles. The dots and dashes of Kantos Kan's reply began coming in immediately.

9

"Your signal comes in perfectly. Tars Tarkas is just leaving the city. The air fleet is mobilizing. The entire air force will stand by to come to your aid. Kantos Kan signing off."

Night found Carter cruising about five hundred miles from Helium. He was very tired. The search of several ruined cities and canals had been fruitless. The buzzing of the microset aroused him again.

"Kantos Kan reporting. Tars Tarkas has organized a complete ground search east to south; other air scouts west to south report nothing. Will acquaint you with any news that might come in. Await orders. Will stand by. Signing off."

"No orders. No news. Carter signing off."

Wearily he let the ship drift. No need to look further until the moons came up. The earthman fell into a fitful sleep.

It was midnight when the speaker sounded, jerking Carter to wakefulness. Kantos Kan was signalling again, excitedly.

"Tars Tarkas has found Dejah Thoris. She is held in a deserted city on the banks of the dead sea at Korvas." Kantos Kan gave the exact latitude and longitude of the spot.

"Further instructions from Tars Tarkas request the greatest secrecy in your movements. He will be at the main bridge leading into the City. Kantos Kan signing off. Come in, John Carter."

John Carter signed off with Kantos Kan, urging him to stand by constantly to be ready with the Helium Air Fleet. Now he set his gyro-compass, a device that would automatically steer him to his destination.

Several hours later, the earthman flew over a low range of hills and saw below him an ancient city on the banks of the Dead Sea. He circled his plane and dropped to the bridge where he had been instructed to meet Tars Tarkas. Long, black shadows filled a dry gully below him.

Carter climbed out of his plane, keeping to the shadows, and made his way to the towering ruins of the city. It was so quiet that a lonely bat swooping from a tower sounded like a falling airship.

Where was Tars Tarkas? The green man should have appeared at the bridge.

At the entrance to the city, Carter stepped into the black shadow of a wall and waited. No sound broke the stillness of the quiet night. The city was like a tomb. Diemos and Phobos, the two fast-moving moons of Mars, whirled across the heavens.

Carter stopped breathing to listen. To his keen ears came the faint sound of steps—strange, shuffling steps dragging closer.

Something was coming along the wall. The earthman tensed, ready to spring away to his ship. Now he could hear other steps all around him. Inside the ruins something dragged against the fallen rocks.

Then a great, heavy body dropped on John Carter from the wall above. Hot, fetid breath burned his neck. Huge, shaggy arms smothered him in their fierce embrace.

The thing hurled him to the rough cobblestones. Huge hands clutched at his throat. Carter turned his head and saw above him the face of a great, white ape.

Three of the creature's fellows were circling around Carter, striving to tie his feet with a piece of rope while the other choked him into insensibility with his four mighty hands.

Carter wriggled his feet under the belly of the ape with whom he was grappling. One mighty heave sent the creature into the air to fall, groaning and helpless, to the ground.

Like a cornered banth,* Carter was on his feet,

* A banth is the huge, eight-legged lion of Mars.—ED.

11

crouched against the wall, awaiting the attacking trio, with drawn sword.

They were mighty beasts, fully eight feet tall with long, white hair covering their great bodies. Each was equipped with four muscular arms that ended in tremendous hands armed with sharp, hooked claws. They were baring their fangs and growling viciously as they came toward the earthman.

Carter crouched low; and as the beasts sprang in, his earthly muscles sent him leaping high into the air over their heads. The earthman's heavy blade backed by all the power of his muscles, smacked down upon one ape's head, splitting the skull wide open.

Carter hit the ground and, turning, was ready when the two apes remaining flew at him again. There was a hideous, hair-raising shriek as this time the earthman's sword sank deep into a savage heart.

As the monster sprawled to the ground, the earthman jerked free his sword.

Now the other beast turned and slunk away in fright, his eyes gleaming at Carter in the darkness as it fled down a long corridor in the adjacent building. The earthman could have sworn that he heard his own name coming from the ape's throat and mingling with its sullen growl as it fled away.

The earthman had just seized his sword when he felt a rush of air above his head. There was a blur of motion as something came down toward him.

Now he felt himself clutched about the waist; then he was jerked fifty feet into the air. Struggling for breath, Carter clutched at the thing encircling his body. It was as horny as the skin of an arbok. It had hairs as large as tree roots bristling from the horny scales. *It was a giant hand!*

THREE

Joog, the Giant

JOHN CARTER found himself looking into a monstrous face.

From top of shaggy head to bottom of its hairy chin, the head measured fully fifteen feet.

A new monstrosity had come to life on Mars. Judging by the adjacent buildings, the creature must have been a hundred and thirty feet tall!

The giant raised Carter high over his head and shook him; then he threw back his face. Hideous, hollow laughter rumbled out of his pendulous lips revealing teeth like small mountain crags.

He was dressed in an ill-fitting, baggy tunic that came down in loose folds over his hips but which allowed his arms and legs to be free.

With his other hand he beat his mighty chest.

"I, Joog. I, Joog," he kept repeating as he continued to laugh and shake his helpless victim. "I can kill! I can kill!"

Joog, the giant, commenced to walk. Carefully he stepped along the barren streets, sometimes going around a building that was too high to step over.

Finally he stopped before a partially ruined palace. The ravages of time had only dimmed its beauty. Huge masses of moss and vines trailed through the masonry, hiding the shattered battlements. With a sudden thrust, Joog, the giant, shoved John Carter through a high window in the palace tower.

When Carter felt the giant's hold releasing upon him he relaxed completely. He hit the stone floor in a long roll, protecting his head with his arms. As he lay in the deep darkness of the place where he had fallen, the earthman listened while he regained his breath.

No sound came to his ears for some time; then he began to hear the heavy breathing of Joog outside his window. Once more Carter's earthly muscles, reacting to the lesser gravity of Mars, sent him leaping twenty feet to the sill of the narrow window. Here he clung and looked once again into the hairy, hideous face of the giant.

"I, Joog. I, Joog," he mumbled. "I can kill! I can kill!" The giant's breath swept over Carter like a blast from a sulphur furnace. There would be no escape from that window!

Once more he dropped down into his cell. This time he commenced a slow circuit of the room, groping his way along the polished ersite slabs that formed the wall. The cobblestone floor was thick with debris. Once, Carter heard the sinister hiss of a Martian spider as he brushed its web.

How long he groped his way around the walls, there was no way of knowing. It seemed hours. Then, suddenly, the deathly silence was shattered by a woman's scream coming from somewhere in the building.

John Carter could feel his skin grow cold. Could that have been the voice of Dejah Thoris?

Once again John Carter leaped toward the faint light that marked the window ledge. Cautiously, he looked down. Joog lay on his back on the flagstones below, breathing as though he were asleep, his great chest rising five feet with every breath.

Quietly he started to edge his way along a ledge that ran from the window and disappeared into the shadow of an adjoining tower. If he could make that shadow without awakening Joog!

He had almost gained his objective when Joog growled hoarsely.

He had opened one great eye. Now he reached up and, grabbing Carter by the leg, hurled him into the tower window again.

Wearily, the earthman crawled to the wall of his dark cell and there slumped down against it. That scream haunted his memory. He was tormented by the thought that Dejah Thoris might be in danger.

And where was Tars Tarkas? Pew Mogel must have captured him, too. Carter suddenly sprang to his feet.

One of the ersite slabs at his back had moved! He waited. Nothing came out. Cautiously, he approached the rock and shoved it with his foot. The slab moved slightly inward. Now Carter shoved the stone with all his tremendous strength. Inch by inch he moved it until finally there was room for him to squeeze his body through.

He was still in utter darkness, but his groping fingers revealed to him that he was in a corridor between two walls. Perhaps this was the way out of his prison!

Carefully he shoved the stone back into position, leaving no trace of his disappearance from the room. The corridor in which he found himself was so low that he was forced to crawl on hands and knees. The low corridor had the stench of age, as if it had been unused for a long time.

Gradually the tunnel sloped more and more downward. Many little side-passages branched off from the main tunnel. There was no light, no noise. Only a faint, pungent odor beginning to fill the air.

Now it was growing lighter. The earthman realized that he must be in the subterranean caverns of the palace. The dim light was caused by the phosphorescent radium glow that is used on all Mars for radiation.

The source of this faint light the earthman suddenly discovered. It was shining through a cleft in the wall ahead. Pushing aside another loose stone, John Carter crawled forth into a chamber. He drew in his breath sharply.

Facing him was a warrior with drawn sword, the point of which was almost touching the breast of the earthman!

John Carter leaped back with the speed of lightning, whipped out his own sword and struck at the other's weapon.

The arm of the red man fell from his body to the floor where it dissolved into dust. The ancient sword clattered on the cobblestones.

Carter could see now that the warrior had been leaning against the wall, balanced there precariously for ages, his sword arm extending in front of him just as it had stiffened long ago in death. The loss of the arm overbalanced the torso which toppled to the floor and there dissolved into a heap of ash-like dust!

In an adjoining chamber there were a score of women, beautiful girls, chained together by collars of gold around their necks. They sat at a table where they had been eating, and the food was still before them. They had been the prisoners, the slaves of the rulers of the long-dead city. The dry, motionless air combined with some gaseous secretion from the walls and dungeons had preserved their beauty through the ages.

The earthman had traversed some little distance down a musty corridor when he became aware of something scraping behind him. Whirling into a side corridor he looked back. Gleaming eyes were coming toward him. They followed him as he backed into the tunnel.

Now again came the scraping, repeated this time farther ahead in the tunnel. Other eyes shone ahead of him.

John Carter ran forward, his sword-point extended. The eyes ahead retreated, but those in back of him started to close in.

It was very dark now, but far ahead the earthman could see a faint gleam of light filtering into the tunnel.

He ran toward the light. Fighting the things where he could see them would be a lot easier than stumbling around in a dark corridor.

Carter entered the room and in the dim light came face to face with the creature whose eyes he had seen ahead of him in the tunnel. It was a species of the huge three-legged Martian rat!

It's yellow fangs were bared hideously in a vicious snarl, as it backed slowly away from Carter to the far end of the small room.

Now behind him came the other rat, and together the two beasts started to close in upon the earthman.

Carter smiled grimly as he gripped his sword.

"I am the proverbial cornered rat now," he muttered as he swung his blade at the nearest creature.

It ducked the blow and scurried toward him.

But the earthman's sword was ready. The charging rat lunged full upon the waiting sword-point.

The momentum of the beast carried Carter back five feet; but he still retained a hold on his sword, the point of which had plunged through the animal's single shoulder and pierced its wild heart.

When Carter had jerked free his sword and turned to meet his other antagonist an exclamation of dismay escaped his lips.

The room was half filled with rats!

The creatures had entered through another opening and had formed a circle around him, waiting to attack.

For half an hour, Carter battled furiously for his life in the lonely dungeon beneath the palace in the ancient city of Korvas.

The carcasses of the dead rats were piled high around him, but still they came and eventually they overpowered him by their very numbers.

John Carter went down by a terrific blow to his head from a snake-like tail.

He was half stunned, but he still clung tenaciously to his sword as he felt himself seized by the arms and dragged away into the darkness of an adjoining tunnel.

FOUR

The City of Rats

JOHN CARTER RECOVERED FULLY when he was dragged through a pool of muddy water. He heard the rats greedily drinking, saw their green eyes gleaming in the darkness. The smell of freshly dug earth reached his nostrils and he realized that he was in a burrow far under the subterranean vaults of the palace.

Several rats on either side of him had hold of his arms by their forepaws as they dragged him along. It was very uncomfortable, and he wondered how much longer the journey would last.

Nor had he long to wait. The strange company finally came out into a huge underground cavern. Light from the outside filtered down through various openings in the ceiling above, its rays reflecting on thousands of gleaming stalactites of red sand stone. Massive stalagmites, huge sedimentary formations of grotesque shape, rose up from the floor of the cavern.

Among these formations on the floor were numerous domeshaped mud huts.

As Carter was dragged by, he stared at a hut that several rats were constructing. The framework was composed of white sticks of various shapes plastered with mud from an underground stream bed. The white sticks were very irregular in length and size. One of the rats stopped work to gnaw at a stick. It looked like a bone.

As he was dragged closer, he saw that the stick was a human thigh bone!

The mud huts were studded with bones and skulls, upon some of which were still dangling hideously the vestiges of hair and skin. Carter noticed that the tops of all the skulls had been removed, neatly sliced off.

The earthman was dragged to a clearing in the center of the cavern. Here, upon a mound of skulls, sat a rat half again as large as the others.

The baleful, pink eyes of the creature glared at Carter as he was dragged up on top of the mound.

The beasts released their hold upon the earthman and descended to the bottom of the mound, leaving Carter alone with the large rat.

The long whiskers of the monster were constantly twitching as the thing sniffed at the man. It had lost one ear in some battle long ago and the other was bright with scar-tissue.

Its little pink eyes surveyed Carter for a long time while it fondly caressed its long, hairless tail with its one claw-like paw.

This, evidently, was the King of the Rats.

"Lord of the Underworld," Carter thought, trying to hold his breath. The stench in the cavern was overwhelming.

Without taking his eyes from Carter's, the rat reached down and picked up a skull beside him and put it in front of Carter. This he repeated, picking up a skull from the other side and placing it beside the first. By repeating this, he eventually formed a little ring of topless heads in front of the earthman.

Now, very judiciously, he climbed inside the circle of skulls and picking one of them up tossed it to Carter. The earthman caught it and tossed it back at the king.

This seemed to annoy his royal highness. He made no effort to catch the skull and it flew past him and went bouncing down the mound.

Instead, the king leaped up and down inside the little circle of skulls, at the same time emitting angry squeals.

This was all very puzzling to the earthman. As he stood there, he became aware of two circles of rats forming at the base of the mound, each circle consisting of about a thousand animals. They began a weird dance, moving around the raised dais of bones counter-clockwise. The tail of each rat was gripped in the mouth of the following beast, thus forming a continuous chain.

There was no doubt that the earthman was in the center of a weird ritual. While he was ignorant of the exact nature of the ceremony, he had little doubt as to its final outcome. The countless barren skulls, the yellowed ones that filled the cavern were mute, horrible evidence of his final fate.

Where did the rats get all the bodies from which the skulls were obtained and why were the tops of those skulls missing? The City of Korvas, as every Martian schoolboy knew, had been deserted for a thousand years; yet many of the skulls and bones were recently picked clean of their flesh. Carter had seen no evidence in the city of any life other than the great white apes and the mysterious giant, and the rats themselves.

However, there had been the woman's scream that he had heard earlier. This thought accentuated his ever-present anxiety over Dejah Thoris's safety and whereabouts.

This delay was tormenting. As the circles of rats

closed in about him, the earthman's eyes eagerly searched for some avenue of escape.

The rats circled slowly, watching their king who rose to his hind legs stamping his feet, thumping his tail. The mound of skulls echoed hollowly.

Faster danced the king and faster moved the circles of rats drawing ever closer to the mound.

The closer rats shot hungry glances at the earthman. Carter smiled grimly and gripped his sword more tightly. Strange that they should let him retain it.

More than one of the beasts would die before he was overcome, and the king would be the first to go. There was no doubt that he was to be sacrificed to furnish a gastronomic orgy.

Suddenly the king stopped his wild gyrations directly in front of Carter. The dancers halted instantly, watching, waiting.

A strange, growling squeal started deep in the king's throat and grew in volume to an ear-piercing shriek. The King of Rats stepped over the ring of skulls and advanced slowly toward Carter.

Once again the earthman glanced about seeking some means of escape from the mound. This time he looked up. The ceiling was at least fifty feet away. No native-born Martian would ever consider escaping in that direction.

But John Carter had been born on the planet Earth, and he had brought with him to Mars all the strength and agility of a trained athlete.

It was upon this, combined with the lesser gravity of Mars, that the earthman made his quick plan for the next moment.

Tensely he waited for his opportunity. The ceremony was nearly concluded. The king was baring his fangs not a foot from Carter's neck.

The earthman's hand tightened on his sword-hilt;

then the blade streaked from its scabbard. There was a blur of motion and a sickening smack. The king's head flew into the air and then rolled away, bouncing down the mound.

The other beasts beneath were stunned into silence, but only momentarily. Now, squealing wildly, they swarmed up the mound intent on tearing the earthman to pieces.

John Carter crouched and with a mighty leap his earthly muscles sent him shooting fifty feet up into the air.

Desperately he clutched and held to a hanging stalactite. Soon he was swinging on the hanging moss to the vast upper reaches of the cavern.

Once he looked down to see the rats milling and squealing in confusion beneath. One other fact he noted, also. Apparently there was only one means of entrance or exit into the dungeon that formed the rats' underground city, the same tunnel through which he had first been dragged.

Now, however, the earthman was intent upon finding some means of exit in the ceiling above.

At last he found a narrow opening; and plunging through a heavy curtain of moss Carter swung into a cave.

There were several tunnels branching off into the darkness, most of them thickly hung with the sticky webs of the great Martian spider. They were evidently parts of a vast underground network of tunnels that had been fashioned long ages ago by the ancients who once inhabited Korvas.

Carter was ready with his blade for any encounter with man or beast that might come his way; and so he started off up the largest tunnel.

The perpetually burning radium light that had been set in the wall when the tunnel was constructed furnished sufficient illumination for the earthman to see his way quite clearly.

Carter halted before a massive door set into the end of a tunnel. It was inscribed with hieroglyphics unfamiliar to the earthman. The subdued drone of what sounded like many motors seemed to come from somewhere beyond the door.

He pushed open the unbarred door and halted just beyond, staring unbelievingly at the tremendous laboratory in which he found himself.

Great motors pumped oxygen through low pipes into rows of glass cages that lined the walls and filled the antiseptically white chamber from end to end. In the center of the laboratory were several operating tables with large searchlights focused down upon them from above.

But the contents of the glass cages immediately absorbed the earthman's attention.

Each cage contained a giant white ape, standing upright inside, apparently lifeless.

The top of each hairy head was swathed in bandages. If these beasts were dead, why then the oxygen tubes running to their cages?

Carter moved across the room to examine the cages at closer range. Halfway to the farther wall he came upon a low, glassed dome that covered a huge pit set in the floor.

He gasped. The pit was filled with dead bodies, red warriors with the tops of their heads neatly sliced off!

FIVE

Chamber of Horrors

FAR BELOW, IN THE PIT, John Carter could see forms moving in and about the bodies of the dead red men.

They were rats; and as he watched, the earthman could see them dragging bodies off into adjoining tunnels. These tunnels probably entered the main one which ran into the rats' underground city.

So this was where the beasts got the skulls and bones with which they constructed their odorous, underground dwellings!

Carter's eyes scanned the laboratory. He noted the operating tables, the encased instruments above, the anesthetics. Everything pointed to some grisly experiment, conducted by some insane scientist.

Within a glass case were many books. One ponderous volume was inscribed in gold letters: PEW MOGEL, HIS LIFE AND WONDERFUL WORKS.

The earthman frowned. What was the explanation?

25

Why this well-equipped laboratory buried in an ancient lost city, a city apparently deserted except for apes, rats, and a giant man?

Why the cages about the wall containing the mute, motionless bodies of apes with bandaged heads? And the red men in the pit—why were their skulls cut in half, their brains removed?

From whence came the giant, the monstrous creature whose likeness had existed only in Barsoomian folklore?

One of the books in a case before Carter bore the name "Pew Mogel." What connection had Pew Mogel with all this and who was the man?

But more important, where was Dejah Thoris, the Princess of Helium?

John Carter reached for Pew Mogel's book. Suddenly the room fell silent. The generators that had been humming out their power, stopped.

"Touch not that book, John Carter," came the words echoing through the laboratory.

Carter's hand dropped to his sword. There was a moment's pause; then the hidden voice continued.

"Give yourself up, John Carter, or your princess dies." The words were apparently coming from a concealed loudspeaker somewhere in the room.

"Through the door to your right, earthman, the door to your right."

Carter immediately sensed a trap. He crossed to the door. Warily, he pushed it open with his foot.

Upon a gorgeous throne at the far end of a huge dome-shaped chamber sat a hideous, misshapen man. A tiny, bullet head squatted upon massive shoulders.

Everything about the creature seemed distorted. His torso was crooked, his arms were not equal in length; one foot was larger than the other.

The face in the diminutive head leered at John

26

Carter. A thick tongue hung partly out over yellowed teeth.

The hulking body was encased in gorgeous trappings of platinum and diamonds. One claw-like hand stroked the bare head.

From head to foot there was apparently not a hair on his body!

At the man's feet crouched a great, four-armed shaggy brute—another white ape. Its little red eyes were fixed steadily upon the earthman as he stood at the far end of the chamber.

The man on the throne idly fingered the microphone with which he had summoned Carter to the room.

"I have trapped you at last, John Carter!" Beady, cocked eyes glared with hatred. "You cannot cope with the great brain of Pew Mogel!"

Pew Mogel turned to a television screen studded with dials and lights of various colors.

His face twisted into a smile. "You honor my humble city, John Carter. It is with the greatest interest I have watched your progress through the many chambers of the palace with my television machine." Pew Mogel patted the machine.

"This little invention of my good teacher, Ras Thavas," continued Pew Mogel, "which I acquired from him, has been an invaluable aid to me in learning of your intended search for my unworthy person. It was unfortunate that you should suspect the honorable intentions of my agent that afternoon in the Jeddak's chambers.

"Fortunately, however, he had already completed his mission; and through an extension upon this television set, concealed cleverly behind a mirror in the Jeddak's private throne room, I was able to see and hear the entire proceedings."

Pew Mogel laughed vacantly, his little unblinking

27

eyes staring steadily at Carter who remained motionless at the other end of the room.

The earthman could see nothing in the chamber that indicated a trap. The walls and floor were all of grey, polished ersite slabs. Carter stood at one end of a long aisle leading to Pew Mogel's throne.

Slowly he advanced toward Pew Mogel, his hand grasping his sword, the muscles of his arm etched bands of steel.

Halfway down the aisle, the earthman halted. "Where is Dejah Thoris?" His words cut the air.

The microcephalic * head of Pew Mogel cocked to one side. Carter waited for him to speak.

In spite of having the features of a man, Pew Mogel did not look quite human. There was something indescribably repulsive about him, the thin lips, the hollow cheeks, the close-set eyes.

Then Carter realized that those eyes were unblinking. There were no eyelids. The man's eyes could never close.

Pew Mogel spoke coldly. "I am greatly indebted to you for this visit. I was fortunate enough to be able to entertain your princess and your best friend; but I hardly dared to hope you would honor me, too."

Carter's face was expressionless. Slowly he repeated. "Where is Dejah Thoris?"

* A microcephalic head is one possessing a very small brain capacity. It is the opposite of megacephalic, which means a large brain capacity. Generally microcephalia is a sign of idiocy, although in the case of Pew Mogel, the condition did not mean idiocy, but extreme craftiness, and madness, which might indicate that, since Pew Mogel was an artificial, synthetic product of Ras Thavas, one of Mars's most famous scientists, his microcephalia was either caused by a disease, or by inability of the brain to adapt itself to a foreign, ill-fitting cranial cavity. Pew Mogel's head was obviously too small for his body, or for his brain.—Ed.

Pew Mogel leered mockingly.

The earthman advanced toward the throne. The white ape at Pew Mogel's feet growled, the hairs on its neck bristling upright as Pew Mogel flinched slightly.

Again the twisted smile passed over his face as he raised his hand toward John Carter and drawled.

"Have patience, John Carter, and I will show you your princess; but first, perhaps you will be interested in seeing the man who, last night, told you to meet him at the main bridge outside the city."

Pew Mogel hooked one of his fingers over a lever projecting from the golden arm of his throne and slipped it toward himself. A pillar to the left of his throne, half set in the wall, began to revolve slowly.

A giant green man appeared, chained to the pillar. His four mighty arms were strapped securely; and for Pew Mogel's additional safety, several steel chains were wrapped around his body and cinched with massive padlocks. His neck and ankles were also secured with bands of steel, also padlocked.

"Tars Tarkas!" Carter exclaimed.

"Kaor, John Carter," there was a grim smile on Tars Tarkas' face as he replied. "I see our friend here trapped us both the same way; but it took a giant fiftime times my size to hold me while they trussed me in these chains."

"The message you sent me last night—" In a flash, Carter realized the truth. Pew Mogel had faked the messages from Kantos Kan and Tars Tarkas, trapping them both in the city the night before.

"Yes, I sent you both identical messages," said Pew Mogel, "each message apparently from the other. The proper broadcasting length I ascertained from listening to the concealed microphone I had planted in the Jeddak's throne room. Clever, eh?"

Pew Mogel's left eye suddenly popped out of its socket and dangled on his cheek. He took no notice of it, but continued to speak, glancing first at Carter and then at Tars Tarkas with the other eye.

"You have both met Joog," stated Pew Mogel. "One hundred and thirty feet tall, he is all muscle, a product of science, the result of my great brain.

"With my own hands I created him from living flesh, the greatest fighting monster that Barsoom has ever seen.

"I modeled him from the organs, tissues, and bones of ten thousand red men and white apes."

Pew Mogel, becoming aware of his left eye, quickly shoved it back into place.

Tars Tarkas laughed one of his rare laughs.

"Pew Mogel," he said, "you are falling apart. As you claim to have created your giant, so you yourself have been made.

"Unless I miss my guess, John Carter," continued Tars Tarkas, "this freak before us who calls himself a king has, himself, crawled out of a tissue vat!"

Pew Mogel's pallid countenance turned even paler as he leaped to his feet. He struck Tars Tarkas a vicious blow on the face.

"Silence, green man!" he shrieked.

Tars Tarkas only smiled at this insult, ignoring the pain. John Carter's face was a frozen mask. One more blow at his defenseless friend would have sent him at Pew Mogel's throat.

Better to bide his time, he knew, until he learned where Dejah Thoris was hidden.

Pew Mogel sank back upon his throne. The white ape, who had risen, once more squatted down at his master's feet.

Presently Pew Mogel smiled again.

"So sorry," he drawled, "that I lost my temper.

Sometimes I forget that my present appearance reveals the nature of my origin.

"You see, soon I shall have trained one of my apes in the intricate procedure of transferring my marvelous brain into a suitable, handsome body; then no one will guess that I am not like any other normal man on Barsoom."

John Carter smiled grimly at Pew Mogel's words.

"Then you *are* one of Ras Thavas' synthetic men?"

SIX

Pew Mogel

"YES, I AM A SYNTHETIC MAN," answered Pew Mogel slowly. "My brain was the greatest achievement of all the Master Mind's creations.

"For years I was a devoted pupil of Ras Thavas in his laboratories at Morbus. I learned all that the Master could teach me of the secrets of creating living tissue. When I learned from him all that I thought necessary to pursue my plans, I left Morbus. With a hundred synthetic men I escaped over the Great Toonolian Marshes on the backs of malagors, the birds of transport.

"I brought with me all the intricate equipment that I could steal from his laboratories. The rest, I have fashioned here in this ancient deserted city where we finally landed."

John Carter was studying Pew Mogel intently.

"I was tired of being a slave," continued Pew Mogel.

33

"I wanted to rule; and by Issus, I have ruled; and some day I shall rule all Barsoom!"

Pew Mogel's eyes gleamed.

"It was not long before red men gathered in our city, escaped and exiled criminals. Since their faces would only lead them to capture and execution in other civilized cities on Barsoom, I persuaded them to allow me to transfer their brains in the bodies of the stupid white apes that overran this city.

"I promised to later restore their brains into the bodies of other red men, provided they would help me in my conquests."

Carter recalled the apes with the bandaged heads in the adjoining laboratory, and the red men with their skulls sliced off in the chamber of the rats. He began to understand a little; then he remembered Joog.

"But the giant?" asked John Carter. "Whence came he?"

Pew Mogel was silent for a minute; then he spoke.

"Joog I have built, piece by piece, during several years, from the bones, tissues and organs of a thousand red men and white apes who came voluntarily to me or whom I captured.

"Even his brain is the synthesis of the brains of ten thousand red men and white apes. Into Joog's veins I have pumped a serum that makes all tissues self-repairing.

"My giant is practically indestructible. No bullet or cannon-shot made can stop him!"

Pew Mogel smiled and stroked his hairless chin.

"Think how powerful my ape soldiers will be," he purred, "each one armed with the great strength of an ape. With their four arms they can hold twice as many weapons as ordinary men, and inside their skulls will function the cunning brains of human beings.

"With Joog and my army of white apes, I can go forth and become master of all Barsoom." Pew Mogel paused and then added, "—provided I acquire more iron for even greater weapons than I already have."

Now Pew Mogel had risen from his throne in his great excitement.

"I preferred to conquer peacefully by first acquiring the Helium iron works as payment for Dejah Thoris's safe return. But the Jeddak and John Carter force me into other alternatives—

"However, I'll give you one more chance to settle peacefully," he said.

Pew Mogel's hand moved toward the right arm of his throne, as he pulled a duplicate lever. A beautiful woman swung into view.

It was Dejah Thoris!

At the sight of his princess chained to the other pillar before him, John Carter grew very pale. He sprang forward to free her.

His earthly muscles could have easily covered the distance in one leap; but halfway there in his spring, Dejah Thoris and Tars Tarkas saw the earthman sprawl in mid-air as though he had struck full force against some invisible barrier. Half-stunned, he crumpled to the floor.

Dejah Thoris gave a little cry. Tars Tarkas strained at his bonds. Slowly, the earthman rose to his feet, shaking his body like some majestic animal. With his sword he reached down and felt the barrier that stood between him and the throne.

Pew Mogel laughed harshly.

"You are trapped, John Carter. The invisible glass partition that you struck is another invention of the great Ras Thavas that I acquired. It is invulnerable.

"From there, you may watch the torture of your princess, unless she sees fit to sign a note to her grandfather demanding the surrender of Helium to me."

The earthman looked at his princess not ten feet from him. Dejah Thoris held her head proudly high, which was answer enough to Pew Mogel's demands that she betray her people.

Pew Mogel saw, and angrily issued a command to the ape. The white brute rose and ambled over to Dejah Thoris. Grabbing her hair with one paw, he forced her head back until he could see her face. His hideous, grinning face was not two inches from hers.

"Demand Helium's surrender," hissed Pew Mogel, "and you shall have your freedom!"

"Never!" the word shot back at him.

Pew Mogel flung another command to the ape.

The creature planted his great, pendulous lips on those of the princess. Dejah Thoris went limp in his embrace, while Tars Tarkas surged vainly at the steel chains. The girl had fainted.

The earthman again hurled himself futilely against the barrier that he could not see.

"Fool," yelled Pew Mogel, "I gave you your chance to retain your princess by turning over to me the Helium iron works; but you and the Jeddak thought you could thwart me and regain Dejah Thoris without paying me the price I asked for her safe return. For that mistake, you all die."

Pew Mogel again reached over to the instrument board beside his throne. He began to turn several dials, and Carter heard a strange, droning noise that increased steadily in volume.

Suddenly the earthman turned and raced for the door through which he came.

But before he had covered fifteen feet, another barrier had closed down. Escape through the door was impossible.

There was a window over on the wall to his right. He leaped for it. He struck another glass barrier.

There was another window on the left side of the room. He had nearly reached it when he was met by another wall of invisible glass.

In a flash he became acutely conscious of his predicament. The walls were moving in upon him. He could see now that the glass barriers had moved out from cleverly concealed slits in the adjoining walls.

The two side barriers, however, were fastened to horizontal pistons in the ceiling. These pistons were moving together, bringing the glass walls toward each other, and would eventually crush the earthman between them.

Upon John Carter's finger was a jeweled ring. Set in the center of the ring was a large diamond.

Diamonds can cut glass!

Here was a new type of glass, but the chances were it was not as hard as the diamond on Carter's finger!

The earthman clenched his fist, pressed the diamond ring against the barrier in front of him and quickly made a large circular scratch in the glass surface.

Then he crashed his body with all his strength against the area of glass enclosed by the scratch.

The section broke out neatly at the blow, and the earthman found himself face to face with Pew Mogel.

Dejah Thoris had regained consciousness, a set, intent expression on her beautiful face. A grim smile had settled over Tars Tarkas's lips when he saw that his friend was no longer impeded by the invisible barriers.

Pew Mogel shrank back on his throne and gasped in a cracked voice.

"Seize him, Gore, seize him!" Little beads of sweat stood forth on his brow.

Gore, the white ape, released his hold on Dejah Thoris and, turning, saw the earthman advancing toward them. Gore snarled viciously, revealing jagged, mighty fangs. He crouched low, so that his four massive fists supported his weight on the floor. His little, beady, blood-shot eyes gleamed hatred, for Gore hated all men save Pew Mogel.

SEVEN

The Flying Terror

As GORE, THE GREAT WHITE APE with a man's brain crouched to meet John Carter, he was fully confident of overcoming his puny man opponent.

But to make assurance doubly sure, Gore drew the great blade at his side and rushed madly at his foe, hacking and cutting viciously.

The momentum of the brute's attack forced Carter backward a few steps as he deftly warded off the mighty blows.

But the earthman saw his chance. Quickly, surely, his blade streaked. There was a sudden twist and Gore's sword went hurtling across the room.

Gore, however, reacted with lightning speed. With his four huge hands he grasped the naked steel of the earthman's sword.

Violently he jerked the blade from Carter's grasp

and, raising it overhead, snapped the strong steel in two as if it had been a splinter of wood.

Now, with a low growl, Gore closed in; and Carter crouched.

Suddenly the man leaped over the ape's head; but again with uncanny speed the monster shot out a hairy hand and grasped the earthman's ankle.

Gore held John Carter in his four hands, drawing the man closer and closer to the drooling jowls and gleaming fangs.

But with a surge of his mighty muscles, the earthman jerked free his arm and sent a terrific blow crashing full into Gore's face.

The ape recoiled, dropping John Carter, and staggered back toward the huge window on the right wall by Pew Mogel's throne.

Here the beast tottered; and the earthman, seeing his chance, once again leaped into the air, but this time flew feet foremost toward the ape.

At the moment of contact with the ape's chest, Carter extended his legs violently; and so, as his feet struck Gore, this force was added to the hurtling momentum of his body.

With a bellowing cry, Gore hurtled out through the window and his screams ended only when he landed with a sickening crunch in the courtyard far below.

Dejah Thoris and Tars Tarkas, chained to the pillars, had watched the short fight, fascinated by the earthman's sure, quick actions.

But when Carter did not succumb instantly to Gore's attack, Pew Mogel had grown frightened. He began jerking dials and switches; and then spoke swiftly into the little microphone beside him.

So now, as the earthman regained his feet and advanced slowly toward Pew Mogel, he did not see the black shadow that obscured the window behind him.

Only when Dejah Thoris screamed a warning did the earthman turn.

But he was too late!

A giant hand, fully three feet across, closed about his body. He was lifted from the floor and pulled out quickly through the window.

To Carter's ears came the hopeless cry of his princess mingled with the cruel, hollow laugh of Pew Mogel.

Carter did not need the added assurance of his eyes to know that he was being held in the grasp of Pew Mogel's synthetic giant. Joog's fetid breath blasting across his face was ample evidence.

Joog held Carter several feet from his face and contracted his features in the semblance of a grin, exposing his two great rows of cracked, stained teeth the size of sharp boulders.

Hoarse, gurgling sounds emanated from Joog's throat as he held the earthman before his face.

"I, Joog. I, Joog," the monster finally managed. "I can kill! I can kill!"

Then he shook his victim until the man's teeth rattled.

But quite suddenly the giant was quiet, listening; then Carter became aware of muffled words coming, apparently, from Joog's ear.

Then John Carter realized that the command was coming from Pew Mogel, transmitted by short wave to a receiving device attached to one of Joog's ears.

"To the arena," repeated the voice. "Fasten him over the pit!"

The pit—what new form of devilish torture was this? Carter tried vaguely to ease the awful pressure that was crushing him.

But his arms were pinned to his sides by the giant's grasp. All the man could do was breathe laboriously and hope that Joog's great strides would soon bring them to his destination, whatever that might be.

The giant's tremendous pace, stepping over tall, ancient edifices or across wide, spacious plazas in single, mighty strides, soon brought them to a large, crowded amphitheatre on the outskirts of the city.

The amphitheatre apparently was fashioned from a natural crater. Row upon row of circular tiers had been carved within the inner wall of the crater, forming a series of levels upon which sat thousands of white apes.

In the center of the arena was a circular pit about fifty feet across. The pit contained what appeared to be water whose level was about fifteen feet from the top of the pit.

Three iron-barred cages hung suspended over the center of the pit by means of three heavy ropes, one attached to the top of each cage and running up through a pulley in the scaffolding built overhead and down to the edge of the pit where it was anchored.

Joog climbed partly over the edge of the coliseum and deposited Carter on the brink of the pit. Five great apes held him there while another ape lowered one of the cages to ground level.

Then he reached out with a hooked pole and swung the cage over the edge. He unlocked the cage door with a large key.

The keeper of the key was a short, heavy-set ape with a bull neck and exceedingly cruel, close-set eyes.

This brute now came up to Carter; and although the captive was being held by five other apes, he grabbed him cruelly by the hair and jerked Carter into the cage, at the same time kicking him viciously.

The cage door was slammed immediately, its padlock bolted closed. Now Carter's cage was pulled up over the pit and the rope end anchored to a davit at the edge.

It was not long before Joog returned with Dejah Thoris and Tars Tarkas. Their chains had been removed.

They were placed in the other two cages that hung over the pit next to that of John Carter.

"Oh, John Carter, my chieftain!" cried Dejah Thoris, when she saw him in the cage next to hers. "Thank Issus you are still alive!" The little princess was crying softly.

John Carter reached through the bars and took her hand in his. He tried to speak reassuring words to her; but he knew, as did Tars Tarkas, who sat grim-faced in the other cage beside his, that Pew Mogel had ordained their deaths—but in what manner they would die, Carter, as yet, was uncertain.

"John Carter," spoke Tars Tarkas softly, "do you notice that all these thousands of apes gathered here in the arena apparently are paying no attention to us?"

"Yes, I noticed," replied the earthman. "They are all looking into the sky toward the city."

"Look," whispered Dejah Thoris. "It's the same thing upon which the ape rode when he captured me in the Helium Forest after shooting our thoat!"

There appeared in the sky, coming from the direction of the city, a great, lone bird upon whose back rode a single man.

The earthman's keen eyes squinted for an instant. "The bird is a malagor. Pew Mogel is riding it."

The bird and its rider circled directly overhead.

"Open the east gate," Pew Mogel commanded, his voice ringing out through a loudspeaker somewhere in the arena. The gates were thrown open and there began pouring out into the arena wave after wave of malagors exactly like the bird Pew Mogel rode.

As the malagors came out, column after column of apes were waiting at the entrance to vault onto the birds' backs. As each bird was mounted, it rose into the air by telepathic command to join a constantly growing formation circling high overhead.

The mounting of the birds must have taken nearly two hours, so great were the number of Pew Mogel's apes and birds. Carter noticed that upon each ape's back was strapped a rifle and each bird itself carried a varying assortment of military equipment, including ammunition supplies, small cannon; and a sub-machine gun was carried by each flight platoon.

At last all was ready and Pew Mogel descended down over the cages of his three captives.

"You see, now, Pew Mogel's mighty army," he cried, "with which he will first conquer Helium and then all Barsoom." The man seemed very confident, for his crooked, misshapen body sat very straight upon his feathered mount.

"Before you are chewed to bits by the reptiles in the rising water below you," he said, "you will have a few moments to consider the fate that awaits Helium within the next forty-eight hours. I should have preferred to conquer peacefully; but you interfered. For that, you die, slowly and horribly."

Pew Mogel turned to the only ape that was left in the arena, the keeper of the key to the cages.

"Open the flood-gate!" was his single command before he rose up to lead his troops off toward the north.

Accompanying the weird, flying army in a sling carried by a hundred malagors rode Joog, the synthetic giant. A hollow, mirthless laugh peeled like thunder from the giant's throat as he was borne away into the sky.

EIGHT

The Reptile Pit

As THE LAST BIRD in Pew Mogel's fantastic army flapped out of sight behind the rim of the crater, John Carter turned to Tars Tarkas in the cage hanging beside him. He spoke softly, so that Dejah Thoris would not hear.

"Those creatures will make Helium a formidable enemy," he said. "Kantos Kan's splendid airfleet and infantry will be hard pressed against those thousands of apes equipped with human brains and modern armament, mounted upon fast birds of prey!"

"Kantos Kan and his airfleet are not even in Helium to protect the city," announced Tars Tarkas grimly. "I heard Pew Mogel bragging that he had sent Kantos Kan a false message, supposedly from you, urging that all Helium's fleet, as well as all ships of the searching party, be dispatched to your aid in the Great Toonolian Marshes."

"The Toonolian Marshes!" Carter gasped. "They're a thousand miles from Helium in the other direction."

A little scream from Dejah Thoris brought the men's attention to their own, immediate fate.

The ape beside the pit had pulled back a tall, metal lever. There was a gurgle of bubbles as air blasted up from the water in the pit below the three captives; and the water at the same time commenced to rise slowly.

The guard now unfastened the rope on each cage and lowered them so that the cage tops were a little below the surface of the ground inside the pit; then he re-fastened the ropes and stood for some time on the brink looking down at the helpless captives.

"The water rises slowly," he sneered thickly; "and so I shall have time now for a little sleep."

It was uncanny to hear words issuing from the mouth of the beast. They were barely articulate, for although the human brain in the ape's skull directed the words, the muscles of the larynx in the creature's throat were normally unequipped for the specialized task of human speech.

The guard lay down on the brink and stretched his massive, squat body.

"Your death cries will awaken me," he mumbled pleasantly, "when the water begins to envelop your feet and the reptiles start clawing at you through the bars of your cages." Whereupon, the ape rolled over and began snoring.

It was then that the three captives saw the slanting, evil eyes, the rows of flashing teeth, in a dozen hideous, reptilian faces staring greedily up at them from the rising waters below.

"Quite ingenious," remarked Tar Tarkas, his stoic face giving no more evidence of fear than did that of the earthman. "When the water partly submerges us, the reptiles will reach in with their claws and begin tearing us to pieces—if there is any life left in us, the

46

rising water will drown it out when it submerges the tops of our cages."

"How horrible!" gasped Dejah Thoris.

John Carter's eyes were fastened on the brink of the pit. From his cage he could just see one of the guard's feet as the fellow lay asleep at the edge of the pit.

Cautioning the others to silence, Carter began swinging his body back and forth while he held fast to the bars of his cage. If he could just get his cage to swinging!—

The water had risen to about ten feet below their cages.

It seemed an eternity before he could get the heavy cage to even moving slightly. Nine feet to the water surface and those hideous, staring eyes and those gleaming teeth!

The cage was swinging now a little more, in rhythm to the earthman's constantly swaying body.

Eight feet, seven feet, six feet came the water. There were about ten reptiles in the water below the captives—ten pairs of narrow, evil eyes fixed steadily to their prey.

The cage was swinging faster.

Five feet, four feet. Tars Tarkas and Dejah Thoris could feel the hot breath of the reptiles!

Three, two feet! Only two more feet to go before the steadily swinging cage would cut into the water and slow down again to a standstill.

But the iron prison, swinging pendulum-like, would reach the brink on its next swing; so this time as the cage moved toward the brink on which lay the sleeping guard, John Carter knew he must act and act quickly!

As the bars of the cage smacked against the cement wall of the pit, John Carter's arms shot out with the quickness of a striking snake.

His fingers closed in a grip of steel about the ankle of the sleeping guard.

An ear-piercing shriek rang out across the arena, echoing dismally in the hollow crater, as the ape felt himself jerked suddenly from his slumbers.

Back swung the cage. Carter regrasped the shrieking ape with his other hand through the bars as they swung out over the water. The reptiles had to lower their heads as the cage moved over them so close had the water risen.

"Good work, John Carter," came Tars Tarkas's tense words as he reached out and grabbed hold of the ape with his four mighty hands. At the same time, Carter's cage splashed to a sudden stop. It had hit the water's surface.

"Hold him, Tars Tarkas, while I pull the key off the scoundrel's neck—there, I've got it!"

The water was flowing over the bottom of the cages. One of the reptiles had reached a horny arm into Dejah Thoris's cage and was attempting to snag her body with its sharp, hooked claws.

Tars Tarkas flung the ape's body with all the force of his giant thews straight at the reptile beside the girl's cage.

"Quickly, John Carter," cried Dejah Thoris. "Save yourself while they are fighting over the ape's body."

"Yes," echoed Tars Tarkas, "unlock your cage and get out while there is still time."

A half-smile lifted the corner of Carter's mouth as he swung open his prison door and leaped to the top of Dejah Thoris's cage.

"I'd sooner stay and die with you both," the earthman said, "than desert you now."

Carter soon had the princess' prison door unlocked;

but as he reached down to lift the girl up, a reptile darted forward into the cage with the princess.

In a quick second, Carter was inside the girl's cage, already knee-deep in water; and he had hurled himself onto the back of the reptile. A steely arm was clamped tightly around the creature's neck. The head was jerked back just in time, for the heavy jaws snapped closed only an inch from the girl's body.

"Climb out, Dejah Thoris—to the top of the cage!" ordered Carter. When the girl had obeyed, Carter dragged the flopping, helpless reptile to the cage door, as other slimy monsters started in. Using its body as a shield before him, the earthman forced his way to the door.

In an instant he had released his hold and vaulted up on top of the cage with the girl.

A moment later he had unlocked Tars Tarkas's cage door. After the green man had swung up beside them without mishap, the three climbed the ropes to the scaffolding above and then lowered themselves down to ground beside the pit.

"Thank Issus," breathed the girl as they sat down to regain their breaths. Her beautiful head was cushioned upon Carter's shoulder, and he stroked her lovely black hair reassuringly.

Presently the earthman rose to his feet. Tars Tarkas had motioned him across the arena.

"There are some malagors left inside here," Tars Tarkas called from the entrance to the cavern inside the crater from where had come Pew Mogel's mounts.

"Good!" exclaimed Carter. "There may be a chance yet to reach and help Helium."

A moment later they had caught two of the birds and had risen over the ancient city of Korvas.

They spotted their planes on the outskirts of the city

where they had left them the night they were tricked into being captured by Pew Mogel.

But to their disappointment, the controls had been destroyed irreparably, so that they were forced to continue their journey on the backs of the malagors.

However, the malagors proved speedy mounts. By noon the next day the trio had reached the City of Thark, inhabited by a hundred thousand green warriors over whom Tars Tarkas ruled.

Gathering the warriors together in the marketplace, Tars Tarkas and John Carter explained the peril that confronted Helium and asked for their support in marching to their allies' aid.

As one man, the mighty warriors shouted their approval. The next day dawned upon a long caravan of thoat-mounted soldiers streaming out from the city gates toward Helium.

A messenger was sent on a malagor to the Toonolian Marshes in an attempt to locate Kantos Kan and urge him to return home with his fleet to aid in the defense of Helium.

Tars Tarkas had abandoned his malagor to this messenger, in favor of a thoat upon which he rode at the head of his warriors. Directly above him, mounted on the other malagor, rode Dejah Thoris and John Carter.

NINE

Attack on Helium

JOHN CARTER AND DEJAH THORIS, mounted upon their malagor, were scouting far ahead of the main column of advancing warriors when they first came into sight of the besieged City of Helium.

It was bright moonlight. The princess voiced a little, disappointed cry when she looked out across the spacious valley toward Helium. Her grandfather's city was completely surrounded by the besieging troops of Pew Mogel.

"My poor city!" The girl was crying softly, for in the bright moonlight below could be easily discerned the terrific gap in the ramparts and the many crushed and shattered buildings of the beautiful metropolis.

John Carter telepathically commanded the malagor to land upon a high peak in the mountains overlooking the Valley of Helium.

"Listen," cautioned John Carter. Pew Mogel's light

entrenched cannon and small arms were commencing to open fire again by moonlight. "They are getting ready for an air attack."

Suddenly, from behind the low foothills between the valley and the towering peaks, there rose the vast, flying army of Pew Mogel.

"They are closing in from all sides," Dejah Thoris cried.

The great winged creatures and their formidable ape riders were swooping down relentlessly upon the city. Only a few of Helium's airships rose to give battle.

"Kantos Kan must have taken nearly all Helium's fleet with him," the earthman remarked. "I am surprised Helium has withstood the attack as long as this."

"You should know my people by now, John Carter," replied the princess.

"The infantry and anti-aircraft fire entrenched in Helium are doing well," Carter replied. "See those birds plummet to the ground."

"They can't hold out much longer, though," the girl replied. "Those apes are dropping bombs squarely into the city, as they swoop over, wave after wave of them —oh, John Carter, what can we do?"

John Carter's old fighting smile, usually present at times of personal danger, had given way to a stern, grave expression.

He saw below him the oldest and most powerful city on Mars being conquered by Pew Mogel's forces. Armed with Helium's vast resources, the synthetic man would go forth and conquer all civilized nations on Mars.

Fifty thousand years of Martian learning and culture wrecked by a power-mad maniac—himself the synthetic product of civilized man!

"Is there nothing we can do to stop him, John Carter?" came the girl's repeated question.

"Very little, I'm afraid, my princess," he replied

sadly. "All we can do is station Tars Tarkas's green warriors at advantageous points in preparation for a counterattack and trust to fate that our messenger reached Kantos Kan in time that he may return and aid us.

"Without supporting aircraft, our green warriors, heroic fighters that they are, can do little against Pew Mogel's superior numbers in the air."

When John Carter and Dejah Thoris returned to Tars Tarkas, they reported what they had seen.

The great Thark agreed that his wariors could avail but little in a direct attack against Pew Mogel's air force. It was decided that half their troops be concentrated at one point and at dawn attempt to rush through into the City.

The remaining half of the warriors would scatter into the mountains in smaller groups and engage the enemy in guerrilla warfare.

Thus they hoped to forestall the fate of Helium until Kantos Kan returned with his fleet of speedy air fighters.

"Helium's fleet of trim, metal fighting craft will furnish Pew Mogel's feathered bird brigade a worthy enemy," remarked Tars Tarkas.

"Provided, of course," added Carter, "Kantos Kan's fleet reaches Helium before Pew Mogel has entrenched himself in the City and returned his own anti-aircraft guns upon them."

All that night in the mountains, under cover of semi-darkness, John Carter and Tars Tarkas reorganized and restationed their troops. By dawn all was ready.

John Carter and Tars Tarkas would lead the advance half of the Tharks in a wild rush toward the gates of Helium; the other half would remain behind, covering their comrades' assault with long-range rifles.

Much against the earthman's will, Dejah Thoris insisted she would ride into the city beside him upon their malagor.

It was just commencing to grow brighter.

"Prepare to charge," Carter ordered. Tars Tarkas passed the word down by his orderly to his unit commanders.

"Prepare to charge! Prepare to charge!" echoed down and across the battalions of magnificent, four-armed, green fighters astride their eight-legged, massive, restless thoats.

The minutes dragged by as the troop lines swung around. Steel swords were drawn from scabbards. Hammers, on short, deadly ray-pistols, clicked back as they cocked over saddle pommels.

John Carter looked around at the girl sitting so straight and steady behind him.

"You are very brave, my princess," he said.

"It's easy to be brave," she replied, "when I'm so close to the greatest warrior on Mars."

"Charge!" came Carter's terse, sudden order.

Down the mountain and across the plain toward Helium streaked the savage horde of Tharks. Out ahead raced Tars Tarkas, his sword held high.

Far ahead and above, on speedy wings, streaked the malagor carrying John Carter and the Princess of Helium.

"John Carter, thank Issus!" Dejah Thoris cried in relief, and pointed toward the far mountain skyline.

"The Helium Fleet has returned," shouted John Carter. "Our messenger reached Kantos Kan in time!" Over the mountains, with flying banners streaming, sailed the mighty Helium Fleet.

There was a moment's silence in the entrenched guns of the enemy. They had seen the charging Tharks and the Helium Fleet simultaneously.

A great cry of triumph rose from the ranks of the

charging warriors at sight of the Helium Fleet streaking to their aid.

"Listen," cried Dejah Thoris to Carter, "the bells of Helium are tolling our victory song!" Then it seemed as though all of Pew Mogel's guns broke loose at once; and from behind the protecting hills rose his flying legions of winged malagors. Upon their backs rode the white apes with men's brains.

Down upon the legions of Tharks came wave after wave of Pew Mogel's feathered squadrons. In true blitzkrieg fashion, the birds would swoop down just out of sword's reach over the green warriors. As each bird pulled out of its dive, the ape on its back would empty its death-dealing atomgun into the mass of warriors beneath.

The carnage was terrific. Only after Tars Tarkas and John Carter had led their warriors into the first lines of entrenched apes did the Tharks find an enemy with whom they could fight effectively.

Here, the four-armed green soldiers of Thark fought gloriously against the great white apes of Pew Mogel's ghastly legions.

But never for a second did the horrible death-diving squadrons cease their attacks from above. Like angry hornets, the thousands dove, killed, climbed, dove, and killed again—always killing.

John Carter masterfully controlled his frightened bird while he issued orders and directed attacks from his vantage point immediately above the center of battle.

Bravely, efficiently, the Princess of Helium protected her chieftain against countless side and rear attacks from the air. The barrel of her radium pistol was red-hot with constant firing; and many were the charging birds and shrieking apes she sent catapulting into the melee below.

Suddenly a hoarse shout rose again from Pew Mogel's legions on ground and in air.

"What is it, my chieftain?" cried the girl. "Why are the enemy shouting in triumph?"

John Carter looked toward the advancing ships now over the mountains only a half mile away; then his blood ran cold.

"The giant—Joog, the giant!"

The creature had risen up from behind the shelter of a low hill, as the ships approached above him. The giant grasped a huge tree trunk in his mighty hand.

Even from where they were, John Carter could discern the head of a man sitting in an armor-enclosed, steel howdah strapped to the top of Joog's helmet.

From the giant's lips there suddenly issued a thunderous, shrieking roar that echoed in the mountains and across the plain.

Then he clambered swiftly to the top of a small hill, before the astonished Heliumites could swerve their speeding craft, the giant struck out mightily with the great tree trunk.

The great, synthetic muscles of Pew Mogel's giant swung the huge weapon full into the advancing craft.

The vanguard of twenty ships, the pride of Helium's airfleet met the blow head-on—went smashing and shattering against the mountain-side, carrying their crews to swift, crushing death!

TEN

Two Thousand Parachutes

KANTOS KAN'S FLAGSHIP narrowly escaped annihilation at the first blow of the giant. The creature's club only missed the leading ship by a few feet.

From their position on the malagor, John Carter and Dejah Thoris could see many of the airships turning back toward the mountains. Others, however, were not so fortunate.

Caught in the wild rush of air resulting from the giant's swinging club, the craft pitched and tossed crazily out of control.

Again and again the huge tree trunk split through the air as the giant swung blow after blow at the helpless ships.

"Kantos Kan is re-forming his fleet," John Carter shouted above the roar of battle as the fighting on the ground was once more resumed with increased zeal.

"The ships are returning again," cried the princess, "toward that awful creature!"

"They are spreading out in the air," the earthman replied. "Kantos Kan is trying to surround the giant!"

"But why?"

"Look, they are giving him some of Pew Mogel's own medicine!"

Helium's vast fleet of airships was darting in from all sides. Others came zooming down from above. As they approached within range of their massive target, the gunners would pour out a veritable hail of bullets and rays into the giant's body.

Dejah Thoris sighed in relief.

"He can't stand that much longer!" she said.

John Carter, however, shook his head sadly as the giant began to strike down the planes with renewed fury.

"I'm afraid it's useless. Not only those bullets but the ray-guns as well are having no effect upon the creature. His body has been imbued with a serum that Ras Thavas discovered. The stuff spreads throughout the tissue cells and makes them grow immediately with unbelievable speed to replace all wounded or destroyed flesh."

"You mean," Dejah Thoris asked, horror-stricken, "the awful monster might never be destroyed?"

"It is probable that he will live and grow forever," replied the earthman, "unless something drastic is done to destroy him—"

A sudden fire of determination flared in the earthman's steel grey eyes.

"There may be a way yet to stop him, my princess, and save our people—"

A weird, bold plan had formulated itself in John Carter's mind. He was accustomed to acting quickly on sudden impulse. Now he ordered his malagor down close over Tars Tarkas's head.

Although he knew the battle was hopeless, the green man was fighting furiously on his great thoat.

"Call your men back to the mountains," shouted Carter to his old friend. "Hide out there and reorganize—wait for my return!"

The next half hour found John Carter and the girl beside Kantos Kan's flagship. The great Helium Fleet had once more retreated over the mountains to take stock of its losses and re-form for a new attack.

Every ship's captain must have known the futility of further battle against this indomitable element; yet they were all willing to fight to the last for their nation and for their princess, who had so recently been rescued.

After the earthman and the girl boarded the flagship, they freed the great malagor that had so faithfully served them. Kantos Kan joyously greeted the princess on bended knee and then welcomed his old friend.

"To know you two are safe again is a pleasure that even outweighs the great sadness of seeing our City of Helium fall into the enemy's hands," stated Kantos Kan sincerely.

"We have not lost yet, Kantos Kan," said the earthman. "I have a plan that might save us—I'll need ten of your largest planes manned by only a minimum crew."

"I'll wire orders for them to break formation and assemble beside the flagship immediately," replied Kantos Kan, turning to an orderly.

"Just a minute," added Carter. "I'll want each plane equipped with *two hundred parachutes!*"

"Two hundred parachutes?" echoed the orderly. "Yes, sir!"

Almost immediately there were ten large aircraft, empty troop ships, drifting in single file formation beside Kantos Kan's flagship. Each had a minimum crew of ten men and two hundred parachutes, two thousand parachutes in all!

Just before he boarded the leading ship, John Carter spoke to Kantos Kan.

"Keep your fleet intact," he said, "until I return. Stay near Helium and protect the city as best you can. I'll be back by dawn."

"But that monster," groaned Kantos Kan. "Look at him—we must do something to save Helium."

The enormous creature, standing one hundred and thirty feet tall, dressed in his ill-fitting, baggy tunic, was tossing boulders and bombs into Helium, his every action dictated through short wave by Pew Mogel, who sat in the armored howdah atop the giant's head.

John Carter laid his hand on Kantos Kan's shoulder.

"Don't waste further ships and men uselessly in fighting the creature," he warned; "and trust me, my friend. Do as I say—at least until dawn!"

John Carter took Dejah Thoris's hand in his and kissed it.

"Goodbye, my chieftain," she whispered, tears filling her eyes.

"You'll be safer here with Kantos Kan, Dejah Thoris," spoke the earthman; and then, "Goodbye my princess," he called and vaulted lightly over the craft's rail to the deck of the troop ship alongside. It pained him to leave Dejah Thoris; yet he knew she was in safe hands.

Ten minutes later, Dejah Thoris and Kantos Kan watched the ten speedy craft disappear into the distant haze.

When John Carter had gone, Kantos Kan unfurled Dejah Thoris's personal colors beside the nation's flag; so that all Helium would know that their princess had been found safe and the people be heartened by her close presence.

During his absence, Kantos Kan and Tars Tarkas followed the earthman's orders, refraining from throwing away their forces in hopeless battle. As a result, Pew Mogel's fighters had moved closer and closer to Helium; while Pew Mogel himself was even now preparing Joog to lead the final assault upon the fortressed city.

Exactly twenty-four hours later, John Carter's ten ships returned.

As he approached Helium, the earthman took in the situation at a glance. He had feared that he would be too late, for his secret mission had occupied more precious time than he had anticipated.

But now he sighed with relief. There was still time to put into execution his bold plan, the plan upon which rested the fate of a nation.

ELEVEN

A Daring Plan

FEARING THAT PEW MOGEL might somehow intercept any shortwave signal to Kantos Kan, John Carter sought out the flagship and hove to alongside it.

The troop ships that had accompanied him on his secret mission were strung out behind their leader.

Their captains awaited the next orders of this remarkable man from another world. In the last twenty-four hours they had seen John Carter accomplish a task that no Martian would have even dreamed of attempting.

The next few hours would determine the success or failure of a plan so fantastic that the earthman himself had half-smiled at its contemplation.

Even his old friend, Kantos Kan, shook his head sadly when John Carter explained his intentions a few minutes later in the cabin of the flagship.

"I'm afraid it's no use, John Carter," he said. "Even

though your plan is most ingeniously conceived, it will avail naught against that horrible monstrosity.

"Helium is doomed, and although we shall all fight until the last to save her, it can do no good."

As he talked, Kantos Kan was looking down at Helium far below. Joog the giant could be seen on the plain hurling great boulders into the city.

Why Pew Mogel had not ordered the giant into the city itself by this time, Carter could not understand— unless it was because Pew Mogel actually enjoyed watching the destructive effect of the boulders as they crashed into the buildings of Helium.

Actually, Joog, however frightful in appearance, could best serve his master's purpose by biding his time, for he was doing more damage at present than he could possibly accomplish within the city itself.

But it was only a matter of time before Pew Mogel would order a general attack upon the city.

Then his entrenched forces would dash in, scaling the walls and crashing the gates. Overhead would swoop the supporting apes on their speedy mounts, bringing death and destruction from the air.

And finally Joog would come, adding the final coup to Pew Mogel's victory.

The horrible carnage that would then fall upon his people made Kantos Kan shudder.

"There is no time to lose, Kantos Kan," spoke the earthman. "I must have your assurance that you will see that my orders are followed to the letter."

Kantos Kan looked at the earthman for some time before he spoke.

"You have my word, John Carter," he said, "even though I know it will mean your death, for no man, not even you, can accomplish what you plan to do!"

"Good!" cried the earthman. "I shall leave immediately; and when you see the giant raise and lower his arm three times, that will be your signal to carry out my orders!"

Just before he left the flagship, John Carter knocked at Dejah Thoris's cabin door.

"Come," he heard her reply from within. As he threw open the door, he saw Dejah Thoris seated at a table. She had just flicked off the visiscreen upon which she had caught the vision of Kantos Kan. The girl rose, tears filling her eyes.

"Do not leave again, John Carter," she pleaded. "Kantos Kan has just told me of your rash plan—it cannot possibly succeed, and you will only be sacrificing yourself uselessly. Stay with me, my chieftain, and we shall die together!"

John Carter strode across the room and took his princess in his arms—perhaps for the last time. She pillowed her head on his broad chest and cried softly. He held her close for a brief moment before he spoke.

"Upon Mars," he said, "I have found a free and kindly people whose civilization I have learned to cherish. Their princess is the woman I love.

"She and her people to whom she belongs are in grave danger. While there is even a slight chance for me to save you and Helium from the terrible catastrophe that threatens all Mars, I must act."

Dejah Thoris straightened a little at his words and smiled bravely as she looked up at him.

"I'm sorry, my chieftain," she whispered. "For a minute, my love for you made me forget that I belong also to my people. If there is any chance of saving them, I would be horribly selfish to detain you; so go now and remember, if you die the heart of Dejah Thoris dies with you!"

A moment later John Carter was seated behind the controls of the fastest, one-man airship in the entire Helium Navy.

He waved farewell to the two forlorn figures who stood at the rail of the flagship.

Then he opened wide the throttle of the quiet, radium engine. He could feel the little craft shudder for an instant as it gained speed. The earthman pointed its nose upward and rose far above the battleground.

Then he nosed over and dove down. The wind whistled shrilly off the craft's trim lines as its increased momentum sped it, comet-like, downward—straight toward the giant!

TWELVE

The Fate of a Nation

NEITHER PEW MOGEL nor the giant Joog had yet seen the lone craft diving toward them from overhead. Pew Mogel, seated inside the armored howdah that was attached to Joog's enormous helmet, was issuing attack orders to his troops by shortwave.

A strip of glass, about three feet wide, completely encircled the howdah, enabling Pew Mogel to obtain complete, unrestricted vision of his fighting forces below.

Perhaps if Pew Mogel had looked up through the circular glass skylight in the dome of his steel shelter, he would have seen the earthman's speedy little craft streaking down on him from above.

John Carter was banking his life, that of the woman he loved and the survival of Helium upon the hope that Pew Mogel would *not* look up.

John Carter was driving his little craft with bullet

speed—straight toward that circular opening on top of Pew Mogel's sanctuary.

Joog was standing still now, shoulders hunched forward. Pew Mogel had ordered him to be quiet while he completed his last-minute command to his troops.

The giant was on the plain between the mountains and the city. Not until he was five hundred feet above the little round window did Carter pull back on the throttle.

He had gained his great height to avoid discovery by Pew Mogel. His speed was for the same purpose.

Now, if he were to come out alive himself, he must slow down his hurtling craft. That impact must occur at exactly the right speed.

If he made the crash too fast, he might succeed only in killing himself, with no assurance that Pew Mogel had died with him.

On the other hand, if the speed of his ship were too slow it would never crash through the tough glass that covered the opening. In that case, his crippled plane would bounce harmlessly off the howdah and carry Carter to his death on the battlefield below.

One hundred feet over the window!

He shut off the motor, a quick glance at the speedometer—too fast for the impact!

His hands flew over the instrument panel. He jerked back on three levers. Three little parachutes whipped out behind the craft. There was a tug on the plane as its speed slowed down.

Then the ship's nose crashed against the little window!

There was a crunch of steel, a splinter of wood, as the ship's nose collapsed; then a clatter of glass that ended in a dull, trembling thud as the craft bore through the window and lodged part way into the floor of Pew Mogel's compartment.

The tail of the craft was protruding out of the top of the howdah, but the craft's door was inside the compartment.

John Carter sprang from his ship, his blade gleaming in his hand.

Pew Mogel was still spinning around crazily in his revolving chair from the tremendous impact. His earphones and attached microphone, with which he had directed Joog's actions as well as his troop formations, had been knocked off his head and lay on the floor at his feet.

When his foolish spin finally stopped, Pew Mogel remained seated. He stared incredulously at the earthman.

His small, lidless eyes bulged. He opened his crooked mouth several times to speak. Now his twisted fingers worked spasmodically.

"Draw your sword, Pew Mogel!" spoke the earthman so low that Pew Mogel could hardly hear the words.

The synthetic man made no move to obey.

"You're dead!" he finally croaked. It was like the man was trying to convince himself that what he saw confronting him with naked sword was only an ill-begotten hallucination. So hard, in fact, did Pew Mogel continue to stare that his left eye behaved as Carter had seen it do once before in Korvas when the creature was excited.

It popped out of its socket and hung down on his cheek.

"Quickly, Pew Mogel, draw your weapon—I have no time to waste!"

Carter could feel the giant below him growing restless, shifting uneasily on his enormous feet. Apparently he did not yet suspect the change of masters in the howdah strapped to his helmet; yet he had jumped perceptibly when Carter's craft had torn into his master's sanctuary.

Carter reached down and picked up the microphone on the floor.

"Raise your arm," he shouted into the mouthpiece.

There was a pause; then the giant raised the right arm high over his head.

"Lower arm," Carter commanded again. The giant obeyed.

Twice more, Carter gave the same command and the giant obeyed each time. The earthman half smiled. He knew Kantos Kan had seen the signal and would follow the orders he had given him earlier.

Now Pew Mogel's hand suddenly shot down to his side. It started back up with a radium gun.

There was a blinding flash as he pulled the trigger; then the gun flew miraculously from his hand.

Carter had leaped to one side. His sword had crashed against the weapon knocking it from Pew Mogel's grasp.

Now the man was forced to draw his sword.

There, on top of the giant's head, fighting furiously with a synthetic man of Mars, John Carter found himself in one of the weirdest predicaments of his adventurous life.

Pew Mogel was no mean swordsman. In fact, so furious was his first attack that he had the earthman backing around the room hard-pressed to parry the swift torrent of blows that were aimed indiscriminately at every inch of his body from head to toe.

It was a ghastly sensation, fighting with a man whose eye hung down the side of his face. Pew Mogel had forgotten that it had popped out. The synthetic man could see equally well with either eye.

Now Pew Mogel had worked the earthman over to the window. Just for an instant he glanced out.

An exclamation of surprise escaped his lips.

THIRTEEN

Panic

JOHN CARTER'S EYES FOLLOWED those of Pew Mogel. What he saw made him smile, renewed hope surging over him.

"Look, Pew Mogel!" he cried. "Your flying army is disbanding!"

The thousands of malagors that had littered the sky with their hairy riders were croaking hoarsely as they scattered in all directions. The apes astride their backs were unable to control their wild fright. The birds were pitching off their riders in wholesale lots, as their great wings flapped furiously to escape that which had suddenly appeared in the sky among them.

The cause of their wild flight was immediately apparent.

The air was filled with parachutes!—and dangling from each falling parachute was a three-legged Martian rat—every Martian bird's hereditary foe!

71

In the quick glance that he took, Carter could see the creatures tumbling out of the troop ships into which he had loaded them during his absence of the last twenty-four hours.

His orders were being followed implicitly.

The rats would soon be landing among Pew Mogel's entrenched troops.

Now, however, John Carter's attention returned to his own immediate peril.

Pew Mogel swung viciously at the earthman. The blade nicked his shoulder, the blood flowed down his bronzed arm.

Carter stole another glance down. Those rats would need support when they landed in the trenches.

Good! Tars Tarkas's green warriors were again racing out of the hills, unhindered now by scathing fire from an enemy above.

True, the rats when they landed would attack anything in their path; but the green Tharks were mounted on fleet thoats—the apes had no mounts. No malagor would stay within sight of its most hated enemy.

Pew Mogel was backing up now once more near the window. Out of the corner of his eye, Carter caught sight of Kantos Kan's air fleet zooming down toward Pew Mogel's ape legions far below.

Pew Mogel suddenly reached down with his free hand.

His fingers clutched the microphone that Carter had dropped when Pew Mogel had first rushed at him.

Now the creature held it to his lips and before the earthman could prevent he shouted into it.

"Joog!" he cried. "Kill! Kill! Kill!"

The next second, John Carter's blade had severed Pew Mogel's head from his shoulders.

The earthman dived for the microphone as it fell from the creature's hands; but he was met by Pew

Mogel's headless body as it lunged blindly around the room still wielding its gleaming weapon.

Pew Mogel's head rolled about the floor, shrieking wildly as Joog charged forward to obey his master's last command to kill!

Joog's head jerked back and forth with each enormous stride. John Carter was hurled roughly about the narrow compartment with each step.

Pew Mogel's headless body floundered across the floor, still striking out madly with the sword in its hand.

"You can't kill me. You can't kill me," shrieked Pew Mogel's head, as it bounced about. "I am Ras Thavas's synthetic man. I never die. I never die!"

The narrow entrance door to the howdah had flopped open as some flying object hit against its bolt.

Pew Mogel's body walked vacantly through the opening and went hurtling down to the ground far below.

Pew Mogel's head saw and shrieked in dismay; then Carter managed to grab it by the car and hurl the head out after the body.

He could hear the thing shrieking all the way down; then its cries ceased suddenly.

Joog was now fighting furiously with the weapon he had just uprooted.

"I kill! I kill!" he bellowed as he smacked the huge club against the Helium planes as they drove down over the trenches.

Although the howdah was rocking violently, Carter clung to the window. He could see the rats landing now by the scores, hurling themselves viciously at the apes in the trenches.

And Tars Tarkas's green warriors were there now, also. They were fighting gloriously beside their great, four-armed leader.

But Joog's mighty club was mowing down a hundred

fighters at a time as he swept it close above the ground.

Joog had to be stopped somehow!

John Carter dove for the microphone that was sliding around the floor. He missed it, dove again. This time his fingers held it.

"Joog—stop! Stop!" Carter shouted into the microphone. Panting and growling, the great creature ceased his ruthless slaughter. He stood hunched over, the sullen, glaring hatred slowly dying away in his eyes, as the battle continued to rage at his feet.

The apes were now completely disbanded. They broke over the trenches and ran toward the mountains, pursued by the vicious, snarling rats and the green warriors of Tars Tarkas.

John Carter could see Kantos Kan's flagship hovering near Joog's head.

Fearing that Joog might aim an irritated blow at the craft with its precious cargo, the earthman signalled the ship to remain aloof.

Then his command once again rang into the microphone.

"Joog, lie down. Lie down!"

Like some tired beast of prey, Joog settled down on the ground amid the bodies of those he had killed.

John Carter leaped out of the Howdah onto the ground. He still retained hold of the microphone that was turned to the shortwave receiving set in Joog's ear.

"Joog!" shouted Carter again. "Go to Korvas. Go to Korvas."

The monster glared at the earthman, not ten feet from his face, and snarled.

FOURTEEN

Adventure's End

ONCE AGAIN THE EARTHMAN repeated his command to Joog the giant. Now the snarl faded from his lips and from the brute's chest came a sound not unlike a sigh as he rose to his feet once again.

Turning slowly, Joog ambled off across the plain toward Korvas.

It was not until ten minutes later after the Heliumite soldiers had stormed from their city and surrounded the earthman and their princess that John Carter, holding Dejah Thoris tightly in his arms, saw Joog's head disappear over the mountains in the distance.

"Why did you let him go, John Carter?" asked Tars Tarkas, as he wiped the blood from his blade on the hide of his sweating thoat.

"Yes, why," repeated Kantos Kan, "when you had him in your power?"

John Carter turned and surveyed the battlefield.

"All the death and destruction that has been caused here today was due not to Joog but to Pew Mogel," replied John Carter.

"Joog is harmless, now that his evil master is dead. Why add his death to all those others, even if we could have killed him—which I doubt?"

Kantos Kan was watching the rats disappear into the far mountains in pursuit of the great, lumbering apes.

"Tell me, John Carter," finally he said, a queer expression on his face, "how did you manage to capture those vicious rats, load them into those troop ships and even strap parachutes on them?"

John Carter smiled. "It was really simple," he said. "I had noticed in Korvas, when I was a prisoner in their underground city, that there was only one means of entrance to the cavern in which the rats live—a single tunnel that continued back for some distance before it branched, although there were openings in the ceiling far above; but they were out of reach.

"I led my men down into that tunnel and we built a huge smoke fire with debris from the ground above. The natural draft carried the smoke into the cavern.

"The place became so filled with smoke that the rats passed out by the scores from lack of oxygen, for they couldn't get by the fire in the tunnel—their only means of escape. Later, we simply went in and dragged out as many as we needed to load into our troop ships."

"But the parachutes!" exclaimed Kantos Kan. "How did you manage to get those on their backs or keep them from tearing them off when the creatures finally became conscious?"

"They did not regain consciousness until the last minute," replied the earthman. "We kept the inside cabin of each troop ship filled with enough smoke to keep the rats unconscious all the way to Helium. We had plenty of time to attach the parachutes to their backs. The rats came to in mid-air after my men shoved them out of the ships."

John Carter nodded toward the disappearing creatures in the mountains. "They were very much alive and fighting mad when they hit the ground, as you saw," added the earthman. "They simply stepped out of their parachute harnesses when they landed, and leaped for anyone in sight.

"As for the malagors," he concluded, "they are birds —and birds on both earth and Mars have no love for snakes or rats. I knew those malagors would prefer other surroundings when they saw and smelled their natural enemies in the air around them!"

Dejah Thoris looked up at her chieftain and smiled.

"Was there ever such a man before?" she asked. "Could it be that all earthmen are like you?"

That night all Helium celebrated its victory The streets of the city surged with laughing people. The mighty, green warriors of Thark mingled in common brotherhood with the fighting legions of Helium.

In the royal palace was staged a great feast in honor of John Carter's service to Helium.

Old Tardos Mors, the jeddak, was so choked with feeling at the miraculous delivery of his city from the hands of their enemy and the safe return of his granddaughter that he was unable to speak for some time when he arose at the dining table to offer the kingdom's thanks to the earthman.

But when he finally spoke, his words were couched with the simple dignity of a great ruler. The intense gratitude of these people deeply touched the earthman's heart.

Later that night, John Carter and Dejah Thoris stood alone on a balcony overlooking the royal gardens.

The moons of Mars circled majestically across the

heavens, causing the shadows of the distant mountains to roll and tumble in an ever-changing fantasy over the plain and the forest.

Even the shadows of the two people on the royal balcony slowly merged into one.

SKELETON MEN OF JUPITER

Foreword

Particularly disliking forewords, I seldom read them;
yet it seems that I scarcely ever write a story that I do
not inflict a foreword on my long-suffering readers.
Occasionally I also have to inject a little weather and
scenery in my deathless classics, two further examples
of literary racketeering that I especially deplore in the
writings of others. Yet there is something to be said in
extenuation of weather and scenery, which, together
with adjectives, do much to lighten the burdens of
authors and run their word count.

Still, there is little excuse for forewords; and if this
were my story there would be none. However, it is not
my story, It is John Carter's story. I am merely his
amanuensius.

On guard! John Carter takes his sword in hand.

EDGAR RICE BURROUGHS

ONE

Betrayed

I AM NO SCIENTIST. I am a fighting man. My most beloved weapon is the sword, and during a long life I have seen no reason to alter my theories as to its proper application to the many problems with which I have been faced. This is not true of the scientists. They are constantly abandoning one theory for another one. The law of gravitation is about the only theory that has held throughout my lifetime—and if the earth should suddenly start rotating seventeen times faster than it now does, even the law of gravitation would fail us and we would all go sailing off into space.

Theories come and theories go—scientific theories. I recall that there was once a theory that Time and Space moved forward constantly in a straight line. There was also a theory that neither Time nor Space existed—it was all in your mind's eye. Then came the theory that Time and Space curved in upon themselves.

Tomorrow, some scientist may show us reams and reams of paper and hundreds of square feet of blackboard covered with equations, formulae, signs, symbols, and diagrams to prove that Time and Space curve out away from themselves. Then our theoretic universe will come tumbling about our ears, and we shall have to start all over again from scratch.

Like many fighting men, I am inclined to be credulous concerning matters outside my vocation; or at least I used to be. I believed whatever the scientists said. Long ago, I believed with Flammarion that Mars was habitable and inhabited; then a newer and more reputable school of scientists convinced me that it was neither. Without losing hope, I was yet forced to believe them until I came to Mars to live. They still insist that Mars is neither habitable nor inhabited, but I live here. Fact and theory seem to be opposed. Unquestionably, the scientists appear to be correct in theory. Equally incontrovertible is it that I am correct in fact.

In the adventure that I am about to narrate, fact and theory will again cross swords. I hate to do this to my long-suffering scientific friends; but if they would only consult me first rather than dogmatically postulating theories which do not meet with popular acclaim, they would save themselves much embarrassment.

Dejah Thoris, my incomparable princess, and I were sitting upon a carved ersite bench in one of the gardens of our palace in Lesser Helium when an officer in the leather of Tardos Mors, Jeddak of Helium, approached and saluted.

"From Tardos Mors to John Carter, kaor!" he said. "The jeddak requests your immediate presence in the Hall of Jeddaks in the imperial palace in Greater Helium."

"At once," I replied.

"May I fly you over, sir?" he asked. "I came in a two-seater."

"Thanks," I replied. "I'll join you at the hangar in a moment." He saluted and left us.

"Who was he?" asked Dejah Thoris. "I don't recall ever having seen him before."

"Probably one of the new officers from Zor, whom Tardos Mors has commissioned in the Jeddak's Guard. It was a gesture of his, made to assure Zor that he has the utmost confidence in the loyalty of that city and as a measure for healing old wounds."

Zor, which lies about three hundred eighty miles southeast of Helium, is one of the more recent conquests of Helium and had given us a great deal of trouble in the past because of treasonable acts instigated by a branch of its royal family led by one Multis Par, a prince. About five years before the events I am about to narrate occurred, this Multis Par had disappeared; and since then Zor had given us no trouble. No one knew what had become of the man, and it was supposed that he had either taken the last, long voyage down the river Iss to the Lost Sea of Korus in the Valley Dor or had been captured and murdered by members of some horde of savage Green men. Nor did anyone appear to care—just so he never returned to Zor, where he was thoroughly hated for his arrogance and cruelty.

"I hope that my revered grandfather does not keep you long," said Dejah Thoris. "We are having a few guests for dinner tonight, and I do not wish you to be late."

"A few!" I said. "How many? Two hundred or three hundred?"

"Don't be impossible," she said, laughing. "Really, only a few."

"A thousand, if it pleases you, my dear," I assured

her as I kissed her. "And now, good-by! I'll doubtless be back within the hour." That was a year ago!

As I ran up the ramp toward the hangar on the palace roof, I had, for some then unaccountable reason, a sense of impending ill; but I attributed it to the fact that my tête-à-tête with my princess had been so quickly interrupted.

The thin air of dying Mars renders the transition from day to night startlingly sudden to an earthman. Twilight is of short duration owing to the negligible refraction of the sun's rays. When I had left Dejah Thoris, the sun, though low, was still shining; the garden was in shadow, but it was still daylight. When I stepped from the head of the ramp to that part of the roof of the palace where the hangar was located which housed the private fliers of the family, dim twilight partially obscured my vision. It would soon be dark. I wondered why the hangar guard had not switched on the lights.

In the very instant that I realized that something was amiss, a score of men surrounded and overpowered me before I could draw and defend myself. A voice cautioned me to silence. It was the voice of the man who had summoned me into this trap. When the others spoke, it was in a language I had never heard before. They spoke in dismal, hollow monotone—expressionless, sepulchral.

They had thrown me face down upon the pavement and trussed my wrists behind my back. Then they jerked me roughly to my feet. Now, for the first time, I obtained a fairly good sight of my captors. I was appalled. I could not believe my own eyes. These things were not men. They were human skeletons! Black eye sockets looked out from grinning skulls. Bony, skeletal fingers grasped my arms. It seemed to me that I could see every bone in each body. Yet the things were alive! They moved. They spoke. They dragged me toward a strange craft that I had not before noticed. It lay in the shadow of the hangar—long, lean, sinister. It looked like an enormous projectile, with rounded nose and tapering tail.

In the first brief glance I had of it, I saw fins forward below its median line, a long, longitudinal aileron (or so I judged it to be) running almost the full length of the ship, and strangely designed elevator and rudder as part of the empennage assembly. I saw no propellors; but then I had little time for a close examination of the strange craft, as I was quickly hustled through a doorway in its metal side. The interior was pitch dark. I could see nothing other than the faint light of the dying day visible through long, narrow portholes in the ship's side.

The man who had betrayed me followed me into the ship with my captors. The door was closed and securely fastened; then the ship rose silently into the night. No light showed upon it, within or without. However, I was certain that one of our patrol ships must see it; then, if nothing more, my people would have a clew upon which to account for my disappearance; and before dawn a thousand ships of the navy of Helium would be scouring the surface of Barsoom and the air above it in search of me, nor could any ship the size of this find hiding place wherein to elude them.

Once above the city, the lights of which I could see below us, the craft shot away at appalling speed. Nothing upon Barsoom could have hoped to overhaul it. It moved at great speed and in utter silence. The cabin lights were switched on. I was disarmed and my hands were freed. I looked with revulsion, almost with horror, upon the twenty or thirty creatures which surrounded me.

I saw now that they were not skeletons, though they still closely resembled the naked bones of dead men.

Parchmentlike skin was stretched tightly over the bony structure of the skull. There seemed to be neither cartilage nor fat underlying it. What I had thought were hollow eye sockets were deep set brown eyes showing no whites. The skin of the face merged with what should have been gums at the roots of the teeth, which were fully exposed in both jaws, precisely as are the teeth of a naked skull. The nose was but a gaping hole in the center of the face. There were no external ears—only the orifices—nor was there any hair upon any of the exposed parts of their bodies nor upon their heads. The things were even more hideous than the hideous kaldanes of Bantoom—those horrifying spider men into whose toils fell Tara of Helium during that adventure which led her to the country of The Chessmen of Mars; they, at least, had beautiful bodies, even though they were not their own.

The bodies of my captors harmonized perfectly with their heads—parchmentlike skin covered the bones of their limbs so tightly that it was difficult to convince one's self that it was not true bone that was exposed. And so tightly was this skin drawn over their torsos that every rib and every vertebra stood out in plain and disgusting relief. When they stood directly in front of a bright light, I could see their internal organs.

They wore no clothing other than a G string. Their harness was quite similar to that which we Barsoomians wear, which is not at all remarkable, since it was designed to serve the same purpose—supporting a sword, a dagger, and a pocket pouch.

Disgusted, I turned away from them to look down upon the moon bathed surface of my beloved Mars. But where was it! Close to port was Cluros, the farther moon! I caught a glimpse of its surface as we flashed by. Fourteen thousand five hundred miles in a little more than a minute! It was incredible.

The red man who had engineered my capture came

and sat down beside me. His rather handsome face was sad. "I am sorry, John Carter," he said. "Perhaps, if you will permit me to explain, you will at least understand why I did it. I do not expect that you will ever forgive me."

"Where is this ship taking me?" I demanded.

"To Sasoom," he said.

Sasoom! That is the Barsoomian name for Jupiter three hundred and forty-two million miles from the palace where my Dejah Thoris awaited me!

TWO

U Dan

FOR SOME TIME I SAT IN SILENCE, gazing out in the inky black void of space, a Stygian backdrop against which stars and planets shone with intense brilliancy, steady and untwinkling. To port or starboard, above, below, the heavens stared at me with unblinking eyes—millions of white hot, penetrating eyes. Many questions harassed my mind. Had I been especially signalled out for capture? If so, why? How had this large ship been able to enter Helium and settle upon my landing stage in broad daylight? Who was this sad-faced, apologetic man who had led me into such a trap? He could have nothing against me personally. Never, before he had stepped into my garden, had I seen him.

It was he who broke the silence. It was as though he had read my thoughts. "You wonder why you are here, John Carter," he said. "If you will bear with mc, I shall tell you. In the first place, let me introduce myself. I am U Dan, formerly a padwar in the guard of Zu Tith, the Jed of Zor who was killed in battle when Helium overthrew his tyrannical reign and annexed the city.

"My sympathies were all upon the side of Helium, and I saw a brilliant and happy future for my beloved city once she was a part of the great Heliumetic empire. I fought against Helium; because it was my sworn duty to defend the jed I loathed—a monster of tyranny and cruelty—but when the war was over, I gladly swore allegiance to Tardos Mors, Jeddak of Helium.

"I had been raised in the palace of the jed in utmost intimacy with the members of the royal family. I knew them all well, especially Multis Par, the prince, who, in the natural course of events, would have succeeded to the throne. He was of a kind with his father, Zu Tith —arrogant, cruel, tyrannical by nature. After the fall of Zor, he sought to foment discord and arouse the people to revolt. When he failed, he disappeared. That was about five years ago.

"Another member of the royal family whom I knew well was as unlike Zu Tith and Multis Par as day is unlike night. Her name is Vaja. She is a cousin of Multis Par. I loved her and she loved me. We were to have been married, when, about two years after the disappearance of Multis Par, Vaja mysteriously disappeared."

I did not understand why he was telling me all this. I was certainly not interested in his love affairs. I was not interested in him. I was still less interested, if possible, in Multis Par; but I listened.

"I searched," he continued. "The governor of Zor gave me every assistance within his power, but all to no avail. Then, one night, Multis Par entered my quarters when I was alone. He wasted no time. He came directly to the point.

" 'I suppose,' he said, 'that you are wondering what has become of Vaja.'

"I knew then that he had been instrumental in her abduction; and I feared the worst, for I knew the type of man he was. I whipped out my sword. 'Where is she?' I demanded. 'Tell me, if you care to live.'

"He only laughed at me. 'Don't be a fool,' he said. 'If you kill me you will never see her again. You will never even know where she is. Work with me, and you may have her back. But you will have to work fast, as I am becoming very fond of her. It is odd,' he added reminiscently, 'that I could have lived for years in the same palace with her and have been blind to her many charms, both mental and physical—especially physical.'

" 'Where is she?' I demanded. 'If you have harmed her, you beast—'

" 'Don't call names, U Dan,' he said. 'If you annoy me too greatly I may keep her for myself and enlist the services of some one other than you to assist me with the plan I had come to explain to you. I thought you would be more sensible. You used to be a very sensible man; but then, of course, love plays strange tricks upon one's mental processes. I am commencing to find that out in my own case.' He gave a nasty little laugh. 'But don't worry,' he continued. 'She is quite safe—so far. How much longer she will be safe depends wholly upon you.'

" 'Where is she?' I demanded.

" 'Where you can never get her without my help,' he replied.

" 'If she is anywhere upon all Barsoom, I shall find her,' I said.

" 'She is not on Barsoom. She is on Sasoom.'

" 'You lie, Multis Par,' I said.

"He shrugged, indifferently. 'Perhaps you will believe her,' he said, and handed me a letter. It was indeed from Vaja. I recall its message word for word:

" 'Incredible as it may seem to you, I am a prisoner on Sasoom. Multis Par has promised to bring you here to me if you will perform what he calls a small favor for him. I do not know what he is going to ask of you; but unless it can be honorably done, do not do it. I am safe and unharmed.' "

"What is it you wish me to do?" I asked.

"I shall not attempt to quote his exact words; but this, in effect, is what he told me: Multis Par's disappearance from Zor was caused by his capture by men from Sasoom. For some time they had been coming to this planet, reconnoitering, having in mind the eventual conquest of Barsoom.

"I asked him for what reason, and he explained that it was simply because they were a warlike race. Their every thought was of war, as it had been for ages until the warlike spirit was as compelling as the urge for self-preservation. They had conquered all other peoples upon Sasoom and sought a new world to conquer.

"They had captured him to learn what they could of the armaments and military effectiveness of various Barsoomian nations, and had decided that as Helium was the most powerful, it would be Helium upon which they would descend. Helium once disposed of, the rest of Barsoom would, they assumed, be easy to conquer."

"And where do I come in in this scheme of theirs?" I asked.

"I am coming to that," said U Dan. "The Morgors are a thorough-going and efficient people. They neglect no littlest detail which might affect the success or failure of a campaign. They already have excellent maps of Barsoom and considerable data relative to the fleets and armament of the principal nations. They now wish to check this data and obtain full information as to the war technique of the Heliumites. This they expect to get from you. This they will get from you."

I smiled. "Neither they nor you rate the honor and loyalty of a Heliumite very highly."

A sad smile crossed his lips. "I know how you feel," he said. "I felt the same way—until they captured Vaja and her life became the price of my acquiescence. Only to save her did I agree to act as a decoy to aid in your capture. The Morgors are adepts in individual and mass psychology as well as in the art of war."

"These things are Morgors?" I asked, nodding in the direction of some of the repulsive creatures. U Dan nodded. "I can appreciate the position in which you have been placed," I said, "but the Morgors have no such hold on me."

"Wait," said U Dan.

"What do you mean?" I demanded.

"Just wait. They will find a way. They are fiends. No one could have convinced me before Multis Par came to me with his proposition that I could have been forced to betray a man whom I, with all decent men, admire as I have admired you, John Carter. Perhaps I was wrong, but when I learned that Vaja would be tortured and mutilated after Multis Par had had his way with her and even then not be allowed to die but kept for future torture, I weakened and gave in. I do not expect you to forgive, but I hope that you will understand."

"I do understand," I said. "Perhaps, under like circumstances, I should have done the same thing." I could see how terribly the man's conscience tortured him. I could see that he was essentially a man of honor. I could forgive him for the thing that he had done for an innocent creature whom he loved, but could he expect me to betray my country, betray my whole world, to save a woman I had never seen. Still, I was bothered. Frankly, I did not know what I should do when faced with the final decision. "At least," I said, "should I ever be situated as you were, I could appear to comply while secretly working to defeat their ends."

"It was thus that I thought," he said. "It is still the final shred by which I cling to my self-respect. Perhaps, before it is too late, I may still be able to save both Vaja and yourself."

"Perhaps we can work together to that end and to the salvation of Helium," I said; "though I am really not greatly worried about Helium. I think she can take care of herself."

He shook his head. "Not if a part, even, of what Multis Par has told me is true. They will come in thousands of these ships, invisible to the inhabitants of Barsoom. Perhaps two million of them will invade Helium and overrun her two principal cities before a single inhabitant is aware that a single enemy threatens their security. They will come with lethal weapons of which Barsoomians know nothing and which they cannot, therefore, combat."

"Invisible ships!" I exclaimed. "Why I saw this one plainly after I was captured."

"Yes," he said. "It was not invisible then, but it was invisible when it came in broad daylight under the bows of your patrol ships and landed in one of the most prominent places in all Lesser Helium. It was not invisible when you first saw it; because it had cast off its invisibility, or, rather, the Morgors had cast it off so that they might find it again themselves, for otherwise it would have been as invisible to them as to us."

"Do you know how they achieve this invisibility?" I asked.

"Multis Par has explained it to me," replied U Dan. "Let me see; I am not much of a scientist, but I think that I recall more or less correctly what he told me. It seems that on some of the ocean beaches on Sasoom there is a submicroscopic, magnetic sand composed of prismatic crystals. When the Morgors desire invisibility for a ship, they magnetize the hull; and then from countless tiny apertures in the hull, they coat the whole exterior of the ship with these prismatic crystals. They simply spray them out, and they settle in a cloud upon the hull, causing light rays to bend around the ship. The instant that the hull is demagnetized, these tiny particles, light as air, fall or are blown off; and instantly the ship is visible again."

Here, a Morgor approached and interrupted our conversation. His manner was arrogant and rude. I could not understand his words, as he spoke his own language in the hollow, graveyard tones I had previously noticed. U Dan replied in the same language but in a less lugubrious tone of voice; then he turned to me.

"Your education is to commence at once," he said, with a wry smile.

"What do you mean?" I asked.

"During this voyage you are to learn the language of the Morgors," he explained.

"How long is the voyage going to last?" I asked. "It takes about three months to learn a language well enough to understand and make yourself understood."

"The voyage will take about eighteen days, as we shall have to make a detour of some million miles to avoid the Asteroids. They happen to lie directly in our way."

"I am supposed to learn their language in eighteen days?" I asked.

"You are not only supposed to, but you will," replied U Dan.

THREE

The Morgors of Sasoon . . .

MY EDUCATION COMMENCED. It was inconceivably brutal, but most effective. My instructors worked on me in relays, scarcely giving me time to eat or sleep. U Dan assisted as interpreter, which was immensely helpful to me, as was the fact that I am exceedingly quick in picking up new languages. Some times I was so overcome by lack of sleep that my brain lagged and my responses were slow and inaccurate. Upon one such occasion, the Morgor who was instructing me slapped my face. I had put up with everything else; because I was so very anxious to learn their language —a vital necessity if I were ever to hope to cope with them and thwart their fantastic plan of conquest. But I could not put up with that. I hit the fellow a single blow that sent him entirely across the cabin, but I almost broke my hand against his unpadded, bony jaw.

He did not get up. He lay where he had fallen. Several of his fellows came for me with drawn swords. The situation looked bad, as I was unarmed. U Dan was appalled. Fortunately for me, the officer in command of the ship had been attracted by the commotion and appeared at the scene of action in time to call his men off. He demanded an explanation.

I had now mastered sufficient words of their language so that I could understand almost everything that was said to me and make myself understood by them, after a fashion. I told the fellow that I had been starved and deprived of sleep and had not complained, but that no man could strike me without suffering the consequences.

"And no creature of a lower order may strike a Morgor without suffering the consequences," he replied.

"What are you going to do about it?" I asked.

"I am going to do nothing about it," he replied. "My orders require me to bring you alive to Eurobus. When I have done that and reported your behavior, it will lie wholly within the discretion of Bandolian as to what your punishment shall be"; then he walked away, but food was brought me and I was allowed to sleep; nor did another Morgor strike me during the remainder of the voyage.

While I was eating, I asked U Dan what Eurobus was. "It is their name for the planet Sasoom," he relied.

"And who is Bandolian?"

"Well, I suppose he would be called a jeddak on Barsoom. I judge this from the numerous references I have heard them make concerning him. Anyhow, he seems to be an object of fear if not veneration."

After a long sleep, I was much refreshed. Everything that I had been taught was clear again in my mind, no longer dulled by exhaustion. It was then that the commander took it upon himself to examine me personally. I am quite sure that he did so for the sole purpose of finding fault with me and perhaps punishing me. He was extremely nasty and arrogant. His simplest questions were at first couched in sarcastic language; but finally, evidently disappointed, he left me. I was given no more instruction.

"You have done well," said U Dan. "You have, in a very short time, mastered their language well enough to suit them."

This was the fifteenth day. During the last three days they left me alone. Travelling through space is stupifyingly monotonous. I had scarcely glanced from the portholes for days. This was, however, principally because my time was constantly devoted to instruction; but now, with nothing else to do, I glanced out. A most gorgeous scene presented itself to my astonished eyes. Gorgeous Jupiter loomed before me in all his majestic immensity. Five of his planets were plainly visible in the heavens. I could even see the tiny one closest to him, which is only thirty miles in diameter. During the ensuing two days. I saw, or at least I thought I saw, all of the remaining five moons. And Jupiter grew larger and more imposing. We were approaching him at the very considerable speed of twenty-three miles per second, but were still some two million miles distant.

Freed from the monotony of language lessons, my mind was once more enslaved to my curiosity. How could life exist upon a planet which one school of scientific thought claimed to have a surface temperature of two hundred and sixty degrees below zero and which another school was equally positive was still in a half molten condition and so hot that gases rose as hot vapor into its thick, warm atmosphere to fall as incessant rain? How could human life exist in an atmosphere made up largely of ammonia and methane gases? And what of the effect of the planet's terrific gravitational pull? Would my legs be able to support my weight? If I fell down, would I be able to rise again?

Another question which presented itself to my mind, related to the motive power which had been carrying us through space at terrific speeds for seventeen days. I asked U Dan if he knew.

"They utilize the Eighth Barsoomian Ray, what we know as the ray of propulsion, in combination with the highly concentrated gravitational forces of all celestial bodies within the range of whose attraction the ship passes, and a concentration of Ray L (cosmic rays) which are collected from space and discharged at high velocities from propulsion tubes at the ship's stern. The eighth Barsoomian Ray helps to give the ship initial velocity upon leaving a planet and as a brake to its terrific speed when approaching its landing upon another. Gravitational forces are utilized both to accelerate speed and to guide the ship. The secret of their success with these inter-planetary ships lies in the ingenious methods they have developed for concentrating these various forces and directing their tremendous energies."

"Thanks, U Dan," I said, "I think I grasp the general idea. It would certainly surprise some of my scientific friends on earth."

My passing reference to scientists started me to thinking of the vast accumulation of theories I was about to see shattered when I landed on Jupiter within the next twenty-four hours. It certainly must be habitable for a race quite similar to our own. These people had lungs, a heart, kidneys, a liver, and other internal organs similar to our own. I knew this for a fact, as I could see them every time one of the Morgors stood between me and a bright light, so thin and transparent was the parchmentlike skin that stretched tightly over their frames. Once more the scientists would be wrong.

I felt sorry for them. They have been wrong so many times and had to eat humble pie. There were those scientists, for instance, who clung to the Ptolemaic System of the universe; and who, after Galileo had discovered four of the moons of Jupiter in 1610, argued that such pretended discoveries were absurd, their argument being that since we have seven openings in the head—two ears, two eyes, two nostrils, and a mouth, there could be in the heavens but seven planets. Having dismissed Galileo's absurd pretensions in this scientific manner, they caused him to be thrown into jail.

When at a distance of about five hundred thousand miles from Jupiter, the ship began to slow down very gradually in preparation for a landing; and some three or four hours later we entered the thick cloud envelope which surrounds the planet. We were barely crawling along now at not more than six hundred miles an hour.

I was all eagerness to see the surface of Jupiter; and extremely impatient of the time that it took the ship to traverse the envelope, in which we could see absolutely nothing.

At last we broke through, and what a sight was revealed to my astonished eyes! A great world lay below me, illuminated by a weird red light which seemed to emanate from the inner surface of the cloud envelope, shedding a rosy glow over mountain, hill, dale, plain, and ocean. At first I could in no way account for this all-pervading illumination; but presently, my eyes roving over the magnificent panorama lying below me, I saw in the distance an enormous volcano, from which giant flames billowed upward thousands of feet into the air. As I was to learn later, the crater of this giant was a full hundred miles in diameter and along the planet's equator there stretched a chain of these Gargantuan torches for some thirty thousand miles, while others were dotted over the entire surface of the globe, giving both light and heat to a world that would have been dark and cold without them.

As we dropped lower, I saw what appeared to be cities, all located at a respectful distance from these craters. In the air, I saw several ships similar to that which had brought me from Mars. Some were very small; others were much larger than the one with which I had become so familiar. Two small ships approached us, and we slowed down almost to a stop. They were evidently patrol ships. From several ports guns were trained on us. One of the ships lay at a little distance; the other came alongside. Our commander raised a hatch in the upper surface of the ship about the control room and stuck his head out. A door in the side of the patrol ship opened, and an officer appeared. The two exchanged a few words; then the commander of the patrol ship saluted and closed the door in which he had appeared. We were free to proceed. All this had taken place at an altitude of some five thousand feet.

We now spiraled down slowly toward a large city. Later, I learned that it covered an area of about four hundred square miles. It was entirely walled, and the walls and buildings were of a uniform dark brown color, as were the pavements of the avenues. It was a dismal, repellent city built entirely of volcanic rock. Within its boundaries I could see no sign of vegetation—not a patch of sward, not a shrub, not a tree; no color to relieve the monotony of somber brown.

The city was perfectly rectangular, having a long axis of about twenty-five miles and a width of about sixteen. The avenues were perfectly straight and equidistant, one from the other, cutting the city into innumerable, identical square blocks. The buildings were all perfect rectangles, though not all of either the same size or height—the only break in the depressing monotony of this gloomy city.

Well, not the only break: there were open spaces

where there were no buildings—perhaps plazas or parade grounds. But these I did not notice until we had dropped quite low above the city, as they were all paved with the same dark brown rock. The city was quite as depressing in appearance as is Salt Lake City from the air on an overcast February day. The only relief from this insistent sense of gloom was the rosy light which pervaded the scene, the reflection of the flames of the great volcanoes from the inner surface of the cloud envelope; this and the riotous growth of tropical verdure beyond the city's walls—weird, unearthly growths of weird unearthly hues.

Accompanied by the two patrol ships, we now dropped gently into a large open space near the center of the city, coming to rest close to a row of hangars in which were many craft similar to our own.

We were immediately surrounded by a detail of warriors; and, much to my surprise, I saw a number of human beings much like myself in appearance, except that their skins were purple. These were unarmed and quite naked except for G strings, having no harness such as is worn by the Morgors. As soon as we had disembarked, these people ran the ship into the hangar. They were slaves.

There were no interchanges of greetings between the returning Morgors and those who had come out to meet the ship. The two commanding officers saluted one another and exchanged a few routine military brevities. The commander of our ship gave his name, which was Haglion, the name of his ship, and stated that he was returning from Mars—he called it Garobus. Then he detailed ten of his own men to accompany him as guards for U Dan and me. They surrounded us, and we walked from the landing field in the wake of Haglion.

He led us along a broad avenue filled with pedestrian and other traffic. On the sidewalks there were only

Morgors. The purple people walked in the gutters. Many Morgors were mounted on enormous, repulsive looking creatures with an infinite number of legs. They reminded me of huge centipedes, their bodies being jointed similarly, each joint being about eighteen inches long. Their heads were piscine and extremely ugly. Their jaws were equipped with many long, sharp teeth. Like nearly all the land animals of Jupiter, as I was to learn later, they were ungulate, hoofs evidently being rendered necessary by the considerable areas of hardened lava on the surface of the planet, as well as by the bits of lava rock which permeate the soil.

These creatures were sometimes of great length, seating as high as ten or twelve Morgors on their backs. There were other beasts of burden on the avenue. They were of strange, unearthly forms; but I shall not bore you by describing them here.

Above this traffic moved small fliers in both directions. Thus the avenue accommodated a multitude of people, strange, dour people who seldom spoke and, as far as I had seen, never laughed. They might have, as indeed they looked, risen from sad graves to rattle their bones in mock life in a cemetery city of the dead.

U Dan and I walked in the gutter, a guard on the sidewalk close beside each of us. We were not good enough to walk where the Morgors walked! Haglion led us to a large plaza surrounded by buildings of considerable size but of no beauty. A few of them boasted towers—some squat, some tall, all ugly. They looked as though they had been built to endure throughout the ages.

We were conducted to one of these buildings, before the entrance to which a single sentry stood. Haglion spoke to him, and he summoned an officer from the interior of the building, after which we all entered. Our names and a description of each of us were entered in a large book. Haglion was given a receipt for us, after which he and our original escort left.

Our new custodian issued instructions to several warriors who were in the room, and they hustled U Dan and me down a spiral stairway to a dim basement, where we were thrown into a gloomy cell. Our escort locked the door on us and departed.

FOUR

. . . And the Savators

ALTHOUGH I had often wondered about Jupiter, I had never hoped nor cared to visit it because of the inhospitable conditions which earthly scientists assure us pertain to this great planet. However, here I was, and conditions were not at all as the scientists had described. Unquestionably, the mass of Jupiter is far greater than that of earth or Mars, yet I felt the gravitational pull far less than I had upon earth. It was even less than that which I had experienced upon Mars. This was due, I realized, to the rapid revolution of the planet upon its axis. Centrifugal force, tending to throw me off into space, more than outweighed the increased force of gravitation. I had never before felt so light upon my feet. I was intrigued by contemplation of the height and distances to which I might jump.

The cell in which I found myself, while large, precluded any experiments along that line. It was a large room of hard, brown lava rock. A few white lights set in recesses in the ceiling gave meager illumination. From the center of one wall a little stream of water tinkled into a small cavity in the floor, the overflow being carried off by a gutter through a small hole in the end wall of the cell. There were some grass mats on the floor. These constituted the sole furnishings of the bleak prison.

"The Morgors are thoughtful hosts," I remarked to U Dan. "They furnish water for drinking and bathing. They have installed sewage facilities. They have given us whereon to lie or sit. Our cell is lighted. It is strong. We are secure against the attacks of our enemies. However, as far as the Morgors are concerned, I—"

"S-s-sh!" cautioned U Dan. "We are not alone." He nodded toward the far end of the cell. I looked, and for the first time perceived what appeared to be the figure of a man stretched upon a mat.

Simultaneously, it arose and came toward us. It was, indeed a man. "You need have no fear of me," he said. "Say what you please of the Morgors. You could not possibly conceive any terms of opprobrium in which to describe them more virulent than those which I have long used and considered inadequate."

Except that the man's skin was a light blue, I could not see that he differed materially in physical appearance from U Dan and myself. His body, which was almost naked, was quite hairless except for a heavy growth on his head and for eyebrows and eyelashes. He spoke the same language as the Morgors. U Dan and I had been conversing in the universal language of Barsoom. I was surprised that the man had been able to understand us. U Dan and I were both silent for a moment.

"Perhaps," suggested our cell mate, "you do not understand the language of Eurobus—eh?"

110

"We do," I said, "but we were surprised that you understood our language."

The fellow laughed. "I did not," he said. "You mentioned the Morgors, so I knew that you were speaking of them; and then, when your companion discovered me, he warned you to silence; so I guessed that you were saying something uncomplimentary about our captors. Tell me—who are you? You are no Morgors, nor do you look like us Savators."

"We are from Barsoom," I said.

"The Morgors call it Garobus," explained U Dan.

"I have heard of it," said the Savator. "It is a world that lies far above the clouds. The Morgors are going to invade it. I suppose they have captured you either to obtain information from you or to hold you as hostages."

"For both purposes, I imagine," said U Dan. "Why are you imprisoned?"

"I accidentally bumped into a Morgor who was crossing an avenue at an intersection. He struck me and I knocked him down. For that, I shall be destroyed at the graduation exercises of the next class."

"What do you mean by that?" I asked.

"The education of the Morgor youth consists almost wholly of subjects and exercises connected with the art of war. Because it is spectacular, because it arouses the blood lust of the participants and the spectators, personal combat winds up the exercises upon graduation day. Those of the graduating class who survive are inducted into the warrior caste—the highest caste among the Morgors. Art, literature, and science, except as they may pertain to war, are held in contempt by the Morgors. They have been kept alive upon Eurobus only through the efforts of us Savators; but, unfortunately, to the neglect of offensive military preparation and training. Being a peace loving people, we armed only

111

for defense." He smiled ruefully and shrugged. "But wars are not won by defensive methods."

"Tell us more about the graduating exercises," said U Dan. "The idea is intriguing. With whom does the graduating class contend?"

"With criminals and slaves," replied the Savator. "Mostly men of my race," he added; "although sometimes there are Morgor criminals of the worst types sentenced to die thus. It is supposed to be the most shameful death that a Morgor can die—fighting shoulder to shoulder with members of a lower order against their own kind."

"Members of a lower order!" I exclaimed. "Do the Morgors consider you that?"

"Just a step above the dumb beasts, but accountable for our acts because we are supposed to be able to differentiate between right and wrong—wrong being any word or act or facial expression adversely critical of anything Morgorian or that can be twisted into a subversive act or gesture."

"And suppose you survive the graduating contest." I asked. "Are you then set at liberty?"

"In theory, yes," he replied; "but in practice, never."

"You mean they fail to honor terms of their own making?" demanded U Dan.

The Savator laughed. "They are entirely without honor," he said, "yet I do not know that they would not liberate one who survived the combat; because, insofar as I know, no one ever has. You see, the members of the class outnumber their antagonists two to one."

This statement gave me a still lower estimate of the character of the Morgors than I had already inferred from my own observation of them. It is not unusual that a warlike people excel in chivalry and a sense of honor; but where all other characteristics are made subservient to brutality, finer humanistic instincts atrophy and disappear.

We sat in silence for some time. It was broken by the Savator. "I do not know your names," he said. "Mine is Zan Dar."

As I told him ours, a detail of Morgor warriors came to our cell and ordered U Dan and me to accompany them. "Good-by!" said Zan Dar. "We probably shall never meet again."

"Shut up, thing!" admonished one of the warriors.

Zan Dar winked at me and laughed. The Morgor was furious. "Silence, creature!" he growled. I thought for a moment that he was going to fall upon Zan Dar with his sword, but he who was in charge of the detail ordered him out of the cell. The incident was but another proof of the egomaniac arrogance of the Morgors. However, it helped to crystallize within me an admiration and liking for the Savator that had been growing since first he spoke to us.

U Dan and I were led across the plaza to a very large building the entrance to which was heavily guarded. The hideous, grinning, skull-like heads of the warriors and their skeletal limbs and bodies, together with the dark and cavernous entrance to the building suggested a grisly fantasia of hell's entrance guarded by the rotting dead. It was not a pleasant thought.

We were held here for quite some time, during which some of the warriors discussed us as one might discuss a couple of stray alley cats. "They are like the Savators and yet unlike them," said one.

"They are quite as hideous," said another.

"One of them is much darker than the other."

Now, for the first time, I was struck by the color of these Morgors. Instead of being ivory color, they were a pink or rosy shade. I looked at U Dan. He was a very dark red. A glance at my arms and hands showed that they, too, were dark red; but not as dark a red as U Dan. At first I was puzzled; then I realized that the reflection of the red glare of the volcanoes from the inner surface of the cloud envelope turned our reddish skins a darker red and made the yellow, parchmentlike skins of the Morgors appear pink. As I looked around, I realized that this same reddish hue appeared upon everything within sight. It reminded me of a verse in the popular song I heard some time ago on one of my visits to earth. It went, I think: "I am looking at the world through rose colored glasses, and everything is rosy now." Well, everything wasn't rosy with me, no matter how rosy this world looked.

Presently an officer came to the entrance and ordered our escort to bring us in. The interior of the building was as unlovely as its exterior. Although this was, as I later learned, the principal palace of the Morgor ruler, there was absolutely no sign of ornamentation. No art relieved the austerity of gloomy, lava-brown corridors and bare, rectangular chambers. No hangings softened the sharp edges of openings; no rugs hid even a part of the bare, brown floors. The pictureless walls frowned down upon us. I have seldom been in a more depressing environment. Even the pits beneath the deserted cities of Barsoom often had interesting vaulted ceilings, arched doorways, elaborate old iron grill work, attesting the artistic temperaments of their designers. The Morgors, like death, were without art.

We were led to a large, bare chamber in which a number of Morgors were clustered about a desk at which another of the creatures was seated. All Morgors look very much alike to me, yet they do have individual facial and physical characteristics; so I was able to recognize Haglion among those standing about the desk. It was Haglion who had commanded the ship that had brought me from Mars.

U Dan and I were halted at some distance from the group, and as we stood there two other red Martians were brought into the room—a man and a girl. The girl was very beautiful.

"Vaja!" exclaimed U Dan, but I did not need this evidence to know who she was. I was equally certain that the man was Multis Par, Prince of Zor. He appeared nervous and downcast, but even so the natural arrogance of the man was indelibly stamped upon his features.

At U Dan's exclamation, one of those guarding us whispered, "Silence, thing!" Vaja's eyes went wide in incredulity as she recognized my companion; and she took an impulsive step toward him, but a warrior seized her arm and restrained her. The faint shadow of a malicious smile touched the thin lips of Multis Par.

The man seated at the desk issued an order, and all four of us were brought forward and lined up in front of him. The fellow differed in appearance not at all from other Morgors. He wore no ornaments. His harness and weapons were quite plain but evidently serviceable. They were marked with a hieroglyph that differed from similar markings on the harness and weapons of the other Morgors, as those of each of the others differed from all the rest. I did not know then what they signified; but later learned that each hieroglyph indicated the name, rank, and title of him who wore it. The hieroglyph of the man at the desk was that of Bandolian, Emperor of the Morgors.

Spread upon the desk before Bandolian was a large map, which I instantly recognized as that of Barsoom. The man and his staff had evidently been studying it. As U Dan and I were halted before his desk with Vaja and Multis Par, Bandolian looked up at the Prince of Zor.

"Which is he," he asked, "who is called Warlord of Barsoom?" Multis Par indicated me, and Bandolian turned his hollow eyes upon me. It was as though Death had looked upon me and singled me out as his own. "I understand that your name is John Carter," he said. I nodded in affirmation. "While you are of a lower order," he continued, "yet it must be that you are endowed with intelligence of a sort. It is to this intelligence that I address my commands. I intend to invade and conquer Barsoom (he called it Garobus), and I command you to give me all the assistance in your power by acquainting me and my staff with such military information as you may possess relative to the principal powers of Garobus, especially that one known as the Empire of Helium. In return for this your life will be spared."

I looked at him for a moment, and then I laughed in his face. The faintest suggestion of a flush overspread the pallor of his face. "You dare laugh at me, thing!" he growled.

"It is my answer to your proposition," I said.

Bandolian was furious. "Take it away and destroy it!" he ordered.

"Wait, Great Bandolian!" urged Multis Par. "His knowledge is almost indispensable to you, and I have a plan whereby you may make use of it."

"What is it?" demanded Bandolian.

"He has a mate whom he worships. Seize her and he will pay any price to protect her from harm."

"Not the price the Morgor has asked," I said to Multis Par, "and if she is brought here it will be the seal upon your death warrant."

"Enough of this," snapped Bandolian. "Take them all away."

"Shall I destroy the one called John Carter?" asked the officer who commanded the detail that had brought us to the audience-chamber.

"Not immediately," replied Bandolian.

"He struck a Morgor," said Haglion; "one of my officers."

"He shall die for that, too," said Bandolian.

"That will be twice," I said.

"Take it away!" snapped Bandolian.

As we were led away, Vaja and U Dan gazed longingly at one another.

FIVE

I Would Be a Traitor

ZAN DAR, THE SAVATOR, was surprised to see us returned to the cell in so short a time. "In fact," he said, "I did not expect ever to see you again. How did it happen?"

I explained briefly what had occurred in the audience chamber, adding, "I have been returned to the cell to await death."

"And you, U Dan?" he asked.

"I don't know why they bothered to take me up there," replied U Dan. "Bandolian paid no attention to me whatever."

"He had a reason, you may rest assured. He is probably trying to break down your morale by letting you see the girl you love, in the belief that you will influence John Carter to accede to his demands. John Carter lives only because Bandolian hopes to eventually break down his resistance."

Time dragged heavily in that cell beneath the Morgor

city. For that matter, there would have been none had we been above ground, for there are no nights upon Jupiter. It is always day. The sun, four hundred eighty-three million miles away, would shed but little light upon the planet even were it exposed to the full light of the star that is the center of our solar system; but that little light is obscured by the dense cloud envelope which surrounds this distant world. What little filters through is negated by the gigantic volcanic torches which bathe the entire planet in perpetual daylight. Although Jupiter rotates upon its axis in less than ten hours, its day is for eternity.

U Dan and I learned much concerning conditions on the planet from Zan Dar. He told us of the vast warm seas which seethed in constant tidal agitation resulting from the constantly changing positions of the four larger moons which revolve about Jupiter in forty-two hours, eighty-five hours, one hundred seventy-two hours, and four hundred hours respectively while the planet spins upon its axis, making a complete revolution in nine hours and fifty-five minutes. He told us of vast continents and enormous islands; and I could well imagine that such existed, as a rough estimate indicated that the area of the planet exceeded twenty-three billion square miles.

As the axis of Jupiter is nearly perpendicular to the plane of its motion, having an inclination of only about 3°, there could be no great variety of seasons; so over this enormous area there existed an equable climate, warm and humid, perpetually lighted and heated by the innumerable volcanoes which pit the surface of the planet. And here was I, an adventurer who had explored two worlds, cooped up in a subterranean cell upon the most amazing and wonderful planet of our entire solar system. It was maddening.

Zan Dar told us that the continent upon which we were was the largest. It was the ancestral home of the

Morgors, from which they had, over a great period of time, sallied forth to conquer the remainder of the world. The conquered countries, each of which was ruled by what might be called a Morgor Governor-General, paid tribute to the Morgors in manufactured goods, foodstuffs, and slaves. There were still a few areas, small and considered of little value by the Morgors, which retained their liberty and their own governments. From such an area came Zan Dar—a remote island called Zanor.

"It is a land of tremendous mountains, thickly forested with trees of great size and height," he said. "Because of our mountains and our forests, it is an easy land to defend against an air borne enemy."

When he told me the height of some of the lofty peaks of Zanor, it was with difficulty that I could believe him: to a height of twenty miles above sea level rose the majestic king of Zanor's mountains.

"The Morgors have sent many an expedition against us," said Zan Dar. "They get a foothold in some little valley; and there, above them and surrounding them in mountain fastnesses that are familiar to us and unknown to them, we have had them at our mercy, picking them off literally one by one until they are so reduced in numbers that they dare remain no longer. They kill many of us, too; and they take prisoners. I was taken thus in one of their invasions. If they brought enough ships and enough men, I suppose they could conquer us; but our land is scarcely worth the effort, and I think they prefer to leave us as we are to give their recruits practice in actual warfare."

"I don't know how long we had been confined when Multis Par was brought to our cell by an officer and a detachment of warriors. He came to exhort me to cooperate with Bandolian.

"The invasion and conquest of Barsoom are inevitable," he said. "By assisting Bandolian you can mitigate the horror of it for the inhabitants of Barsoom. You will thus be serving our world far better than by stupidly and stubbornly refusing to meet Bandolian half way."

"You are wasting your time," I told him.

"But our own lives depend upon it," he cried. "You and U Dan, Vaja and I shall die if you refuse. Bandolian's patience is almost worn out now." He looked pleadingly at U Dan.

"We could not die in a better cause," said U Dan, much to my surprise. "I shall be glad to die in atonement for the wrong that I did John Carter."

"You are two fools!" exclaimed Multis Par, angrily.

"At least we are not traitors," I reminded him.

"You will die, John Carter," he growled; "but before you die, you shall see your mate in the clutches of Bandolian. She has been sent for. Now, if you change your mind, send word by one of those who bring your meals."

I sprang forward and knocked the creature down. I should have killed him then had not the Morgors dragged him from the cell.

So they had sent for Dejah Thoris—and I was helpless. They would get her. I knew how they would get her—by assuring her that only through her co-operation could my immediate death be averted. I wondered if they would win. Would I, in the final test, sacrifice my beloved princess or my adopted country? Frankly, I did not know; but I had the example of U Dan to guide me. He had placed patriotism above love. Would I?

Time dragged on in this gloomy cell where there was no time. We three plotted innumerable futile plans of escape. We improvised games to help mitigate the monotony of our dull existence. More profitably, however, U Dan and I learned much from Zan Dar concerning this great planet. And Zan Dar learned much of what lay beyond the eternal cloud envelope which hides from the view of the inhabitants of Jupiter the sun, the other planets, the stars, and even their own moons. All that Zan Dar knew of them was the little he had been able to glean from remarks dropped by Morgors of what had been seen from their interplanetary ships. Their knowledge of astronomy was only slightly less than their interest in the subject, which was practically non-existent. War, conquest, and bloodshed were their sole interests in life.

At last there came a break in the deadly monotony of our lives: a new prisoner was thrown into the cell with us. And he was a Morgor! The situation was embarrassing. Had our numbers been reversed, had there been three Morgors and one of us, there would have been no doubt as to the treatment that one would have received. He would have been ostracized, imposed upon, and very possibly abused. The Morgor expected this fate. He went into a far corner of the cell and awaited what he had every reason to expect. U Dan, Zan Dar, and I discussed the situation in whispers. That must have been a trying time for the Morgor. We three finally decided to treat the creature simply as a fellow prisoner until such time as his own conduct should be our eventual guide. Zan Dar was the first to break the ice. In a friendly manner he asked what mischance had brought the fellow to this pass.

"I killed one who had an influential relative in the palace of Bandolian," he replied, and as he spoke he came over closer to us. "For that I shall die, probably in the graduating exercises of the next class. We shall doubtless all die together," he added with a hollow laugh. He paused. "Unless we escape," he concluded.

"Then we shall die," said Zan Dar.

"Perhaps," said the Morgor.

"One does not escape from the prisons of the Morgors," said Zan Dar.

I was interested in that one word "perhaps." It seemed to me fraught with intentional meaning. I determined to cultivate this animated skeleton. It could do no harm and might lead to good. I told him my name and the names of my companions; then I asked his.

"Vorion," he replied; "but I need no introduction to you, John Carter. We have met before. Don't you recognize me?" I had to admit that I did not. Vorion laughed. "I slapped your face and you knocked me across the ship. It was a noble blow. For a long time they thought that I was dead."

"Oh," I said, "you were one of my instructors. It may please you to know that I am going to die for that blow."

"Perhaps not," said Vorion. There was that "perhaps" again. What did the fellow mean?

Much to our surprise, Vorion proved not at all a bad companion. Toward Bandolian and the powerful forces that had condemned him to death and thrown him into prison he was extremely bitter. I learned from him that the apparent veneration and loyalty accorded Bandolian by his people was wholly a matter of disciplined regimentation. At heart, Vorion loathed the man as a monster of cruelty and tyranny. "Fear and generations of training hold our apparent loyalty," he said.

After he had been with us for some time, he said to me, "You three have been very decent to me. You could have made my life miserable here; and I could not have blamed you had you done so, for you must hate us Morgors."

"We are all in the same boat," I said. "We could gain nothing by fighting among ourselves. If we work together—perhaps—" I used his own perhaps.

Vorion nodded. "I have been thinking that we might work together," he said.

"To what end?" I asked.

"Escape."

"Is that possible?"

"Perhaps."

U Dan and Zan Dar were eager listeners. Vorion turned to the latter. "If we should escape," he said, "you three have a country to which you might go with every assurance of finding asylum, while I could expect only death in any country upon the face of Eurobus. If you could promise me safety in your country—" He paused, evidently awaiting Zan Dar's reaction.

"I could only promise to do my best for you," said Zan Dar; "but I am confident that if you were the means of my liberation and return to Zanor, you would be permitted to remain there in safety."

Our plotting was interrupted by the arrival of a detail of warriors. The officer in command singled me out and ordered me from the cell. If I were to be separated from my companions, I saw the fabric of my dream of escape dissolve before my eyes.

They led me from the building and across the plaza to the palace of Bandolian, and after some delay I found myself again in the audience chamber. From behind his desk, the hollow eyes of the tyrant stared at me from their grinning skull. "I am giving you your last chance," said Bandolian; then he turned to one of his officers. "Bring in the other," he said. There was a short wait, and then a door at my right opened and a guard of warriors brought in the "other." It was Dejah Thoris! My incomparable Dejah Thoris!

What a lovely creature she was as she crossed the floor surrounded by hideous Morgors. What majestic dignity, what fearlessness distinguished her carriage and her mien! That such as she should be sacrificed even for a world! They halted her scarce two paces from me. She gave me a brave smile, and whispered, "Courage! I know now why I am here. Do not weaken. Better death than dishonor."

"What is she saying?" demanded Bandolian.

I thought quickly. I knew that the chances were that not one of them there understood the language of Barsoom. In their stupid arrogance they would not deign to master the tongue of a lower order.

"She but pleads with me to save her," I said. I saw Dejah Thoris smile. Evidently they had taught her the language of the Morgors on the long voyage from Mars.

"And you will be wise to do so," said Bandolian, "otherwise she will be given to Multis Par and afterward tortured and mutilated many times before she is permitted to die."

I shuddered in contemplation of such a fate for my princess, and in that moment I weakened once again. "If I aid you, will she be returned unharmed to Helium?" I asked.

"Both of you will—after I have conquered Garobus," replied Bandolian.

"No! No!" whispered Dejah Thoris. "I should rather die than return to Helium with a traitor. No, John Carter, you could never be that even to save my life."

"But the torture! The mutilation! I would be a traitor a thousand times over to save you from that, and I can promise you that no odium would be attached to you: I should never return to Barsoom."

"I shall be neither tortured nor mutilated," she said. "Sewn into my harness is a long, thin blade."

I understood and I was relieved. "Very well," I said. "If we are to die for Barsoom, it is no more than thousands of her brave warriors have done in the past; but we are not dead yet. Remember that, my princess; and do not use that long, thin blade upon yourself until hope is absolutely dead."

"While you live, hope will live," she said.

"Come, come," said Bandolian. "I have listened long enough to your silly jabbering. Do you accept my proposition?"

"I am considering it," I said, "but I must have a few more words with my mate."

"Let them be few," snapped the Morgor.

I turned to Dejah Thoris. "Where are you imprisoned?" I asked.

"On the top floor of a tower at the rear of this building at the corner nearest the great volcano. There is another Barsoomian with me—a girl from Zor. Her name is Vaja."

Bandolian was becoming impatient. He drummed nervously on his desk with his knuckles and snapped his grinning jaws together like castanets. "Enough of this!" he growled. "What is your decision?"

"The matter is one of vast importance to me," I replied. "I cannot decide it in a moment. Return me to my cell so that I may think it over and discuss it with U Dan, who also has much at stake."

"Take it back to its cell," ordered Bandolian; and then, to me: "You shall have time, but not much. My patience is exhausted."

SIX

Escape

I HAD NO PLAN. I was practically without hope, yet I had gained at least a brief reprieve for Dejah Thoris. Perhaps a means of escape might offer itself. Upon such unsubstantial fare I fed the shred of hope to which I clung.

My cell mates were both surprised and relieved when I was returned to them. I told them briefly of what had occurred in the audience chamber of Bandolian. U Dan showed real grief when he learned that Dejah Thoris was in the clutches of the Morgors, and cursed himself for the part he had taken in bringing her and me to a situation in which we faced the alternatives of death or dishonor.

"Vain regrets never got anyone anywhere," I said. "They won't get us out of this cell. They won't get Dejah Thoris and Vaja out of Bandolian's tower. Forget them. We have other things to think about." I turned to Vorion. "You have spoken of the possibility of escape. Explain yourself."

He was not accustomed to being spoken to thus peremptorily by one of the lower orders, as the Morgors considered us; but he laughed, taking it in good part. The Morgors cannot smile. From birth to death they wear their death's head grin—frozen, unchangeable.

"There is just a chance," he said. "It is just barely a chance. Slender would be an optimistic description of it, but if it fails we shall be no worse off than we are now."

"Tell us what it is," I said.

"I can pick the lock of our cell door," he explained. "If luck is with us, we can escape from this building. I know a way that is little used, for I was for long one of the prison guard."

"What chance would we have once we were in the streets of the city?" demanded U Dan. "We three, at least, would be picked up immediately."

"Not necessarily," said Vorion. "There are many slaves on the avenues who look exactly like Zan Dar. Of course, the color of the skin of you men from Garobus might attract attention; but that is a chance we shall have to take."

"And after we are in the streets?" asked Zan Dar. "What then?"

"I shall pretend that I am in charge of you. I shall treat you as slaves are so often treated that it will arouse no comment nor attract any undue attention. I shall have to be rough with you, but you will understand. I shall herd you to a field where there are many ships. There I shall tell the guard that I have orders to bring you to clean a certain ship. In this field are only the private ships of the rich and powerful among us, and I well know a certain ship that belongs to one who seldom uses it. If we can reach this ship and board it, nothing

130

can prevent us from escaping. In an hour from now, we shall be on our way to Zanor—if all goes well."

"And if we can take Vaja and Deja Thoris with us," I added.

"I had forgotten them," said Vorion. "You would risk your lives for two females?"

"Certainly," said U Dan.

Vorion shrugged. "You are strange creatures," he said.

"We Morgors would not risk a little finger for a score of them. The only reason that we tolerate them at all is that they are needed to replenish the supply of warriors. To attempt to rescue two of yours may easily end in disaster for us all."

"However, we shall make the attempt," I said. "Are you with us, Zan Dar?" I asked the Savator.

"To the end," he said, "whatever it may be."

Again Vorion shrugged. "As you will," he said, but not with much enthusiasm; then he set to work on the lock, and in a very short time the door swung open and we stepped out into the corridor. Vorion closed the door and relocked it. "This is going to give them food for speculation," he remarked.

He led us along the corridor in the opposite direction from that in which we had been brought to it and from which all those had come who had approached our cell since our incarceration. The corridor became dark and dusty the farther we traversed it. Evidently it was little used. At its very end was a door, the lock to which Vorion quickly picked; and a moment later we stepped out into a narrow alleyway.

So simple had been our escape up to now that I immediately apprehended the worst: such luck could not last. Even the alley which we had entered was deserted: no one had seen us emerge from the prison. But when we reached the end of the alley and turned into a broad avenue, the situation was very different.

Here were many people—Morgors upon the sidewalks, slaves in the gutters, strange beasts of burden carrying their loads of passengers upon the pavement.

Now, Vorion began to berate and cuff as we walked in the gutter and he upon the sidewalk. He directed us away from the central plaza and finally into less frequented avenues, yet we still passed too many Morgors to suit me. At any minute one of them might notice the unusual coloration of U Dan's skin and mine. I glanced at Zan Dar to note if the difference between his coloration and ours was at all startling, and I got a shock. Zan Dar's skin had been blue. Now it was purple! It took me a moment to realize that the change was due to the rosy light of the volcano's flames turning Zan Dar's natural blue to purple.

We had covered quite a little distance in safety, when a Morgor, passing, eyed us suspiciously. He let us go by him; then he wheeled and called to Vorion. "Who are those two?" he demanded. "They are not Savators."

"They have been ill," said Vorion, "and their color has changed." I was surprised that the fellow could think so quickly.

"Well, who are you?" asked the fellow, "and what are you doing in charge of slaves while unarmed?"

Vorion looked down at his sides in simulated surprise. "Why, I must have forgotten them," he said.

"I think that you are lying to me," said the fellow. "Come along with me, all of you."

Here seemed an end of our hopes of escape. I glanced up and down the street. It appeared to be a quiet, residential avenue. There was no one near us. Several small ships rested at the curb in front of drear, brown domiciles. That was all. No eyes were upon us. I stepped close to the fellow who had thus rashly presented himself as an obstacle in the way of Dejah Thoris' rescue. I struck him once. I struck him with all my strength. He dropped like a log.

"You have killed him," exclaimed Vorion. "He was one of Bandolian's most trusted officers. If we are caught now, we shall be tortured to death."

"We need not be caught," I said. "Let's take one of these ships standing at the curb. Why take the time and the risk to go farther?"

Vorion shook his head. "They wouldn't do," he said. "They are only for intramural use. They are low altitude ships that would never get over even a relatively small mountain range; but more important still, they cannot be rendered invisible. We shall have to go on to the field as we have planned."

"To avoid another such encounter as we have just experienced," I said, "we had better take one of these ships at least to the vicinity of the field."

"We shall be no worse off adding theft to murder," said Zan Dar.

Vorion agreed, and a moment later we were all in a small ship and sailing along a few yards above the avenue. Keenly interested, I carefully noted everything that Vorion did in starting the motor and controlling the craft. It was necessary for me to ask only a few questions in order to have an excellent grasp of the handling of the little ship, so familiar was I with the airships of two other worlds. Perhaps I should never have the opportunity to operate one of these, but it could do no harm to know how.

We quitted the flier a short distance from the field and continued on foot. As Vorion had predicted, a guard halted us and questioned him. For a moment everything hung in the balance. The guard appeared skeptical, and the reason for his skepticism was largely that which had motivated the officer I had killed to question the regularity of Vorion's asserted mission— the fact that Vorion was unarmed. The guard told us to wait while he summoned an officer. That would have been fatal. I felt that I might have to kill this man, too;

but I did not see how I could do it without being observed, as there were many Morgors upon the field, though none in our immediate vicinity.

Vorion saved the day. "Come! Come!" he exclaimed in a tone of exasperation. "I can't wait here all day while you send for an officer. I am in a hurry. Let me take these slaves on and start them to work. The officer can come to the ship and question me as well as he can question me here."

The guard agreed that there was something in this; and, after ascertaining the name and location of the ship which we were supposed to clean, he permitted us to proceed. I breathed an inward sigh of relief. After we had left him, Vorion said that he had given him the name and location of a different ship than that which we were planning to steal. Vorion was no fool.

The ship that Vorion had selected, was a slim craft which appeared to have been designed for speed. We lost no time boarding her; and once again I watched every move that Vorion made, questioning him concerning everything that was not entirely clear to me. Although I had spent some eighteen days aboard one of these Morgorian ships, I had learned nothing relative to their control, as I had never been allowed in the control room or permitted to ask questions.

First, Vorion magnetized the hull and sprayed it with the fine sands of invisibility; then he started the motor and nosed up gently. I had explained my plan to him, and once he had gained a little altitude he headed for the palace of Bandolian. Through a tiny lens set in the bow of this ship the view ahead was reflected upon a ground glass plate, just as an image is projected upon the finder of a camera. There were several of these lenses, and through one of them I presently saw the square tower at the rear of the palace, the tower in which Dejah Thoris and Vaja were confined.

"When I bring the ship up to the window," said

Vorion, "you will have to work fast, as the moment that we open the door in the ship's hull, part of the interior of the ship will be visible. Some one in the palace or upon the ground may notice it, and instantly we shall be surrounded by guard and patrol ships."

"I shall work fast," I said.

I must admit that I was more excited than usual as Vorion brought the craft alongside the tower window, which we had seen was wide open and unbarred. U Dan and Zan Dar stood by to open the door so that I could leap through the window and then to close it immediately after I had come aboard with the two girls. I could no longer see the window now that the craft was broadside to it; but at a word from Vorion, U Dan and Zan Dar slid the door back. The open window was before me, and I leaped through it into the interior of the tower room.

Fortunately for me, fortunately for Dejah Thoris, and fortunately for Vaja, it was the right room. The two girls were there, but they were not alone. A man held Dejah Thoris in his arms, his lips searching for hers. Vaja was striking him futilely on the back, and Dejah Thoris was trying to push his face from hers.

I seized the man by the neck and hurled him across the room, then I pointed to the window and the ship beyond and told the girls to get aboard as fast as they could. They needed no second invitation. As they ran across the room toward the window, the man rose and faced me. It was Multis Par! Recognizing me, he went almost white; then he whipped out his sword and simultaneously commenced to shout for the guard.

Seeing that I was unarmed, he came for me. I could not turn and run for the window: had I, he could have run me through long before I could have reached it; so I did the next best thing. I charged straight for him. This apparently suicidal act of mine evidently confused him, for he fell back. But when I was close to him, he lunged for me. I parried the thrust with my forearm. I was inside his point now, and an instant later my fingers closed upon his throat. Like a fool, he dropped his sword then and attempted to claw my fingers loose with his two hands. He could have shortened his hold on it and run me through the heart, but I had had to take that chance.

I would have finished him off in a moment had not the door of the room been then thrown open to admit a dozen Morgor warriors. I was stunned! After everything had worked so well, to have this happen! Were all our plans to be thus thwarted? No, not all.

I shouted to U Dan: "Close the door and take off! It is a command!"

U Dan hesitated. Dejah Thoris stood at his side with one hand outstretched toward me and an indescribable expression of anguish on her face. She took a step forward as though to leap from the ship back into the room. U Dan quickly barred her way, and then the ship started to move away. Slowly the door slid closed, and once again the craft was entirely invisible.

All this transpired in but a few seconds while I still clung to Multis Par's throat. His tongue protruded and his eyes stared glassily. In a moment more he would have been dead; then the Morgor warriors were upon me, and I was dragged from my prey.

My captors handled me rather roughly and, perhaps, not without reason, for I had knocked three of them unconscious before they overpowered me. Had I but had a sword! What I should have done to them then! But though I was battered and bruised as they hustled me down from the tower, I was smiling; for I was happy. Dejah Thoris had been snatched from the clutches of the skeleton men and was, temporarily at least, safe. I had good cause for rejoicing.

I was taken to a small, unlighted cell beneath the tower; and here I was manacled and chained to the wall. A heavy door was slammed shut as my captors left me, and I heard a key turn in a massive lock.

SEVEN

Pho Lar

IN SOLITARY CONFINEMENT unrelieved by even a suggestion of light, one is thrown entirely upon the resources of one's thoughts for mitigation of absolute boredom—such boredom as sometimes leads to insanity for those of weak wills and feeble nerves. But my thoughts were pleasant thoughts. I envisaged Dejah Thoris safely bound for a friendly country in an invisible ship which would be safe from capture, and I felt that three of those who accompanied her would be definitely friendly and that one of them, U Dan, might be expected to lay down his life to protect her were that ever necessary. As to Vorion, I could not even guess what his attitude toward her would be.

My own situation gave me little concern. I will admit that it looked rather hopeless, but I had been in tight places before and yet managed to survive and escape. I still lived, and while life is in me I never give up hope.

I am a confirmed optimist, which, I think, gives me an attitude of mind that more often than not commands what we commonly term the breaks of life.

Fortunately, I was not long confined in that dark cell. I slept once, for how long I do not know; and I was very hungry when a detail of warriors came to take me away, hungry and thirsty, for they had given me neither food nor water while I had been confined.

I was not taken before Bandolian this time, but to one of his officers—a huge skeleton that continually opened and closed its jaws with a snapping and grinding sound. The creature was Death incarnate. From the way he questionted me, I concluded that he must be the lord high inquisitor. In silence, he eyed me from those seemingly hollow sockets for a full minute before he spoke; then he bellowed at me.

"Thing," he shouted, "for even a small part of what you have done you deserve death—death after torture."

"You don't have to shout at me," I said; "I am not deaf."

That enraged him, and he pounded upon his desk. "For impudence and disrespect it will go harder with you."

"I cannot show respect when I do not feel respect," I told him. "I respect only those who command my respect. I surely could not respect a bag of bones with an evil disposition."

I do not know why I deliberately tried to infuriate him. Perhaps it is just a weakness of mine to enjoy baiting enemies whom I think contemptible. It is, I admit, a habit fraught with danger; and, perhaps, a stupid habit; but I have found that it sometimes so disconcerts an enemy as to give me a certain advantage. In this instance I was at least successful in part: the creature was so furious that for some time it remained speechless; then it leaped to its feet with drawn sword.

My situation was far from enviable. I was unarmed,

and the creature facing me was in an uncontrollable rage. In addition to all this, there were four or five other Morgors in the room, two of whom were holding my arms—one on either side. I was as helpless as a sheep in an abattoir. But as my would-be executioner came around the end of his desk to spit me on his blade, another Morgor entered the room.

The newcomer took in the situation at a glance, and shouted. "Stop, Gorgum!" The thing coming for me hesitated a moment then he dropped his point.

"The creature deserves death," Gorgum said, sullenly. "It defied and insulted me—me, an officer of the Great Bandolian!"

"Vengeance belongs to Bandolian," said the other, "and he has different plans for this insolent worm. What has your questioning developed?"

"He has been so busy screaming at me that he has had no time to question me," I said.

"Silence, low one!" snapped the newcomer. "I can well understand," he said to Gorgum, "that your patience must have been sorely tried; but we must respect the wishes of the Great Bandolian. Proceed with the investigation."

Gorgum returned his sword to its scabbard and re-seated himself at his desk. "What is your name?" he demanded.

"John Carter, Prince of Helium," I replied. A scribe at Gorgum's side scribbled in a large book. I supposed that he was recording the question and the answer. He kept this up during the entire interview.

"How did you and the other conspirators escape from the cell in which you were confined?" Gorgum asked.

"Through the doorway," I replied.

"That is impossible. The door was locked when you were placed in the cell. It was locked at the time your absence was discovered."

"If you know so much, why bother to question me?"

Gorgum's jaws snapped and ground more viciously than ever. "You see, Horur," he said angrily, turning to the other officer, "the insolence of the creature."

"Answer the noble Gorgum's question," Horur snapped at me. "How did you pass through a locked door?"

"It was not locked."

"It *was* locked," shouted Gorgum.

I shrugged. "What is the use?" I asked. "It is a waste of time to answer the questions of one who knows more about the subject than I, notwithstanding the fact that he was not there."

"Tell me, then, in your own words how you escaped from the cell," said Horur in a less irritating tone of voice.

"We picked the lock."

"That would have been impossible," bellowed Gorgum.

"Then we are still in the cell," I said. "Perhaps you had better go and look."

"We are getting nowhere," snapped Horur.

"Rapidly," I agreed.

"I shall question the prisoner," said Horur. "We concede that you did escape from the cell."

"Rather shrewd of you."

He ignored the comment. "I cannot see that the means you adopted are of great importance. What we really wish to know is where your accomplices and the two female prisoners are now. Multis Par says that they escaped in a ship—probably one of our own which was stolen from a flying field."

"I do not know where they are."

"Do you know where they planned to go?"

"If I did, I would not tell you."

"I command you to answer me, on pain of death."

I laughed at the creature. "You intend to kill me anyway; so your threat finds me indifferent."

Horur kept his temper much better than had Gorgum, but I could see that he was annoyed. "You could preserve your life if you were more co-operative," he said. "Great Bandolian asks but little of you. Tell us where your accomplices intended going and promise to aid Great Bandolian in his conquest of Helium, and your life will be spared."

"No," I said.

"Wait," urged Horur. "Bandolian will go even further. Following our conquest of Helium, he will permit you and your mate to return to that country and he will give you a high office in the new government he intends to establish there. If you refuse, you shall be destroyed; your mate will be hunted down and, I promise you, she will be found. Her fate will be infinitely worse than death. You had better think it over."

"I do not need to think over such a proposition. I can give you a final answer on both counts—my irrevocable answer. It is—never!"

If Horur had had a lip, he would doubtless have bitten it. He looked at me for a long minute; then he said, "Fool!" after which he turned to Gorgum. "Have it placed with those who are being held for the next class," then he left the room.

I was now taken to a building located at some distance from those in which I had previously been incarcerated, and placed in a large cell with some twenty other prisoners, all of whom were Savators.

"What have we here?" demanded one of my fellow prisoners after my escort had left and locked the door. "A man with a red skin! He is no Savator. What are you, fellow?"

I did not like the looks of him, nor his tone of voice. I was not seeking trouble with those with whom I was to be imprisoned and with whom I was probably destined to die; so I walked away from the fellow and sat down on a bench in another part of the chamber, which was quite large. But the fool followed me and stood in front of me in a truculent attitude.

"I asked you what you were," he said, threateningly; "and when Pho Lar asks you a question, see that you answer it—and quickly. I am top man here." He looked around at the others. "That's right, isn't it?" he demanded of them.

There were some sullen, affirmative grunts. I could see at once that the fellow was unpopular. He appeared a man of considerable muscular development; and his reception of me, a newcomer among them, testified to the fact that he was a bully. It was evident that he had the other prisoners cowed.

"You seem to be looking for trouble, Lo Phar," I said; "but I am not. I am already in enough trouble."

"My name is Pho Lar, fellow," he barked.

"What difference does it make? You would stink by any name." The other prisoners immediately took interested notice. Some of them grinned.

"I see that I shall have to put you in your place," said Pho Lar, advancing toward me angrily.

"I do not want any trouble with you," I said. "It is bad enough to be imprisoned, without quarrelling with fellow prisoners."

"You are evidently a coward," said Pho Lar; "so, if you will get down on your knees and ask my pardon, I shall not harm you."

I had to laugh at that, which made the fellow furious; yet he hesitated to attack me. I realized then that he was a typical bully—yellow at heart. However, to save his face, he would probably attack me if he could not bluff me. "Don't make me angry," he said. "When I am angry I do not know my own strength. I might kill you."

"I wonder if this would make you angry," I said, and slapped him across the cheek with my open palm. I slapped him so hard that he nearly fell down. I could have slapped him harder. This staggered him more than physically. The blood rushed to his blue face until it turned purple. He was in a spot. He had started something; and if he were to hold his self-appointed position as top man, as he had described himself, he would have to finish it. The other prisoners had now all arisen and formed a half circle about us. They looked alternately at Pho Lar and at me in eager anticipation.

Pho Lar had to do something about that slap in the face. He rushed at me and struck out clumsily. As I warded off his blows, I realized that he was a very powerful man; but he lacked science, and I was sure that he lacked guts. I determined to teach him a lesson that he would not soon forget. I could have landed a blow in the first few seconds of our encounter that would have put him to sleep, but I preferred to play with him.

I countered merely with another slap in the face. He came back with a haymaker that I ducked; then I slapped him again—a little harder this time.

"Good work!" exclaimed one of the prisoners.

"Go to it, red man!" cried another.

"Kill him!" shouted a third.

Pho Lar tried to clinch; but I caught one of his wrists, wheeled around, bent over, and threw him over my shoulder. He lit heavily on the lava flooring. He lay there for a moment, and as he scrambled to his feet I put a headlock on him and threw him again. This time he did not get up; so I picked him up and hit him on the chin. He went down for a long count. I was through with him, and went and sat down.

The prisoners gathered around me. I could see that they were pleased with the outcome of the fight. "Pho

Lar's had this coming to him for a long time," said one.

"He sure got it at last!"

"Who are you, anyway?"

"My name is John Carter. I am from Garobus."

"I have heard of you," said one. "I think we all have. The Morgors are furious at you because you tricked them so easily. I suppose they have sent you here to die with us. My name is Han Du." He held out a hand to me. It was the first time that I had seen this friendly gesture since leaving the earth. The Martians place a hand upon your shoulder. I took his hand.

"I am glad to know you, Han Du," I said. "If there are many more here like Pho Lar, I shall probably need a friend."

"There are no more like him," said Han Du, "and he is finished."

"You intimated that you are all doomed to die," I said. "Do you know when or how?"

"When the next class graduates, we shall be pitted against twice our number of Morgors. It will be soon, now."

EIGHT

In the Arena

PHO LAR WAS UNCONSCIOUS FOR A LONG TIME. For a while, I thought that I might have killed him; but finally he opened his eyes and looked about. Then he sat up, felt of his head, and rubbed his jaw. When his eyes found me, he dropped them to the floor. Slowly and painfully he got to his feet and started for the far side of the room. Four or five of the prisoners immediately surrounded him.

"Who's top man now?" demanded one of them and slapped his face. Two more struck him. They were pushing him around and buffeting him when I walked among them and pushed them away.

"Leave him alone," I said. "He has had enough punishment for a while. When he has recovered, if one of you wishes to take him on, that will be all right; but you can't gang up on him."

The biggest of them turned and faced me. "What

have *you* got to say about it?" he demanded.

"This," I replied and knocked him down.

He sat up and looked at me. "I was just asking," he said, and grinned a sickly grin; then everybody laughed and the tension was over. After this, we got along famously—all of us, even Pho Lar; and I found them all rather decent men. Long imprisonment and the knowledge that they were facing death had frayed their nerves; but what had followed my advent had cleared the air, much as a violent electrical storm does. After that there was a lot of laughing and talking.

I inquired if any of them were from Zan Dar's country—Zanor; but none of them was. Several of them knew where it was, and one scratched a rough map of part of Jupiter on the wall of our cell to show me where Zanor was located. "But much good it will do you to know," he said.

"One never can tell," I replied.

They had told me what I was to expect at the graduating exercises, and I gave the subject considerable thought. I did not purpose attending a Morgor commencement in the role of a willing sacrifice.

"How many of you men are expert swordsmen?" I asked.

About half of them claimed to be, but it is a failing of fighting men to boast of their prowess. Not of all fighting men, but of many—usually those with the least to boast of. I wished that I had some means of determining which were really good.

"Of course we can't get hold of any swords," I said, "but if we had some sticks about the length of swords, we could soon find out who were the best swordsmen among us."

"What good would that do us?" asked one.

"We could give those Morgors a run for their money," I said, "and make them pay for their own graduation."

"The slave who brings our food is from my country," said Han Du. "I think he might smuggle a couple of sticks in to us. He is a good fellow. I'll ask him when he comes."

Pho Lar had said nothing about his swordsmanship; so, as he had proved himself a great boaster, I felt that he was not a swordsman at all. I was sorry, as he was by far the most powerful of all the Savator prisoners; and he was tall, too. With a little skill, he should have proved a most formidable swordsman. Han Du never boasted about anything; but he said that in his country, the men were much given to sword play; so I was counting on him.

Finally, Han Du's compatriot smuggled in a couple of wooden rods about the length of a long sword; and I went to work to ascertain how my fellow prisoners stacked up as swordsmen. Most of them were good; a few were excellent; Han Du was magnificent; and, much to everyone's surprise, Pho Lar was superb. He gave me one of the most strenuous workouts I have ever had before I could touch him. It must have taken me nearly an hour to disarm him. He was one of the greatest swordsmen I had ever faced.

Since our altercation upon my induction to their company, Pho Lar had kept much to himself. He seldom spoke, and I thought he might be brooding and planning on revenge. I had to find out just where he stood, as I could not take any chances on treachery or even half-hearted co-operation.

I took Pho Lar aside after the passage with the wooden sticks. I put my cards squarely on the table. "My plan," I said, "requires as many good swordsmen as I can get. You are one of the finest I have ever met, but you may think that you have reason to dislike me and therefore be unwilling to give me your full support. I cannot use any man who will not follow me and obey me even to death. How about it?"

149

"I will follow wherever you lead," he said. "Here is my hand on it—if you will take my hand in friendship."

"I am glad to do it."

As we grasped hands, he said, "If I had known a man like you years ago, I should not have been the fool that I have been. You may count on me to my last drop of blood, and before you and I die we shall have shown the Morgors something that they will never forget. They think that they are great swordsmen, but after they have seen you in action they will have their doubts. I can scarcely wait for the time."

I was impressed by Pho Lar's protestations. I felt that he was sincere, but I could not disabuse my mind of my first impression of him that he was at heart an arrant coward. But perhaps, facing death, he would fight as a cornered rat fights. If he did, and didn't lose his head, he would wreak havoc on the Morgors.

There were twenty of us in that cell. No longer did time drag heavily. It passed quickly in practice with our two wooden rods. Han Du, Pho Lar, and I, acting as instructors, taught the others what tricks of swordsmanship we knew until we were twenty excellent swordsmen. Several were outstanding.

We discussed several plans of action. We knew that, if custom prevailed, we should be pitted against forty young Morgor cadets striving to win to the warrior caste. We decided to fight in pairs, each of our ten best swordsmen being pared with one of the ten less proficient; but this pairing was to follow an initial charge by the first ten, with our team mates close behind us. We hoped thus to eliminate many of the Morgors in the first few moments of the encounter, thus greatly reducing the odds against us. Perhaps we of the first ten overestimated our prowess. Only time would tell.

There was some nervousness among the prisoners,

due, I think, to the uncertainty as to when we should be called upon to face those unequal odds. Each knew that some of us would die. If any survived, we had only rumor to substantiate our hope that they would be set free; and no man there trusted the Morgors. Every footfall in the corridor brought silence to the cell, with every eye fixed upon the door.

At long last our anxiety was relieved: a full company of warriors came to escort us to the field where we were to fight. I glanced quickly around at the prisoners' faces. Many were smiling and there were sighs of relief. I felt greatly encouraged.

We were taken to a rectangular field with tiers of seats on each of its four sides. The stands were crowded. Thousands of eyes stared from the hollow sockets of grinning skulls. It might have been a field day in Hell. There was no sound. There were no bands. There were no flying flags—no color. We were given swords and herded together at one end of the field. An official gave us our instructions.

"When the cadets come on the field at the far end, you will advance and engage them." That was all.

"And what of those of us who survive?" I asked.

"None of you will survive, creature," he replied.

"We understand that those who survive would be given their freedom," I insisted.

"None of you will survive," he repeated.

"Would you like to place a little bet on that?"

"None of your impudence, creature!" The fellow was getting angry.

"But suppose one of us should survive?" I demanded.

"In that case his life would be spared and he would be allowed to continue in slavery, but none has ever survived these exercises. The cadets are on the field!" he cried. "Go to your deaths, worms!"

"To your stations, worms!" I commanded. The prisoners laughed as they took their allotted positions: the first ten in the front line, each with his partner behind him. I was near the center of the line. Han Du and Pho Lar were on the flanks. We marched forward as we had practiced it in our cell, all in step, the men in the rear rank giving the cadence by chanting, "Death to the Morgors!" over and over. We kept intervals and distance a little greater than the length of an extended sword arm and sword.

It was evident that the Morgors had never seen anything like that at a commencement exercise, for I could hear the hollow sound of their exclamations of surprise arising from the stands; and the cadets advancing to meet us were seemingly thrown into confusion. They were spread out in pairs in a line that extended almost all the way across the field, and it suddenly became a very ragged line. When we were about twenty-five feet from this line, I gave the command, "Charge!"

We ten, hitting the center of their line, had no odds against us: the Morgors had spread their line too thin. They saw swordsmanship in those first few seconds such as I'll warrant no Morgor ever saw before. Ten Morgors lay dead or dying on the field, as five of our first ten wheeled toward the right, followed by our partners; and our remaining ten men wheeled to the left.

As we had not lost a man in the first onslaught, each ten was now pitted against fifteen of the enemy. The odds were not so heavily against us. Taking each half of the Morgor line on its flank, as we now were, gave us a great advantage; and we took heavy toll of them before those on the far flanks could get into action, with the result that we were presently fighting on an almost even footing, our partners having now come into action.

The Morgors fought with fanatic determination. Many of them were splendid swordsmen, but none of them was a match for any of our first ten. I caught an occasional glimpse of Pho Lar. He was magnificent. I doubt that any swordsman of any of the three worlds upon which I had fought could have touched Pho Lar, Han Du, or me with his point; and there were seven more of us here almost as good.

Within fifteen minutes of the start of the engagement, all that remained was the mopping up of the surviving Morgors. We had lost ten men, all of the first ten swordsmen having survived. As the last of the Morgors fell, one could almost feel the deathly silence that had settled upon the audience.

The nine gathered around me. "What now?" asked Pho Lar.

"How many of you want to go back to slavery?" I asked.

"No!" shouted nine voices.

"We are the ten best swords on Eurobus," I said. "We could fight our way out of the city. You men know the country beyond. What chance would we have to escape capture?"

"There would be a chance," said Han Du. "Beyond the city, the jungle comes close. If we could make that, they might never find us."

"Good!" I said, and started at a trot toward a gate at one end of the field, the nine at my heels.

At the gateway, a handful of foolish guardsmen tried to stop us. We left them behind us, dead. Now we heard angry shouts arising from the field we had left, and we guessed that soon we should have hundreds of Morgors in pursuit.

"Who knows the way to the nearest gate?" I demanded.

"I do," said one of my companions. "Follow me!" and he set off at a run.

As we raced through the avenues of the drear city, the angry shouts of our pursuers followed us; but we held our distance and at last arrived at one of the city gates. Here again we were confronted by armed warriors who compelled us to put up a stiff battle. The cries of the pursuing Morgors grew louder and louder. Soon all that we had gained would be lost. This must not be! I called Pho Lar and Han Du to my side and ordered the remaining seven to give us room, for the gateway was too narrow for ten men to wield their blades within it advantageously.

"This time we go through!" I shouted to my two companions as we rushed the surviving guardsmen. And we went through. They hadn't a chance against the three best swordsmen of three worlds.

Miraculous as it may seem, all ten of us won to freedom with nothing more than a few superficial scratches to indicate that we had been in a fight; but the howling Morgors were now close on our heels. If there is anything in three worlds that I hate, it is to run from a foe; but it would have been utterly stupid to have permitted several hundred angry Morgors to have overtaken me. I ran.

The Morgors gave up the chase before we reached the jungle. Evidently they had other plans for capturing us. We did not stop until we were far into the tropical verdure of a great forest; then we paused to discuss the future and to rest, and we needed rest.

That forest! I almost hesitate to describe it, so weird, so unearthly was it. Almost wholly deprived of sunlight, the foliage was pale, pale with a deathlike pallor, tinged with rose where the reflected light of the fiery volcanoes filtered through. But this was by far its least uncanny aspect: the limbs of the trees moved like living things. They writhed and twined—myriad, snakelike things. I had scarcely noticed them until we halted. Suddenly one dropped down and wrapped itself about me. Smiling, I sought to disentwine it. I stopped smiling: I was as helpless as a babe encircled by the trunk of an elephant. The thing started to lift me from the ground, and just then Han Du saw and leaped forward with drawn sword. He grasped one of my legs, and at the same time sprang upward and struck with the keen edge of his blade, severing the limb that had seized me. We dropped to the ground together.

"What the devil!" I exclaimed. "What is it? and why did it do that?"

Han Du pointed up. I looked. Above me, at the end of a strong stem, was a huge blossom—a horrible thing! In its center was a large mouth armed with many teeth, and above the mouth were two staring, lidless eyes.

"I had forgotten," said Han Du, "that you are not of Eurobus. Perhaps you have no such trees as these in your world."

"We certainly have not," I assured him. "A few that eat insects, perhaps, like Venus's-flytrap; but no maneaters."

"You must always be on your guard when in one of our forests," he warned me. "These trees are living, carnivorous animals. They have a nervous system and a brain, and it is generally believed that they have a language and talk with one another."

Just then a hideous scream broke from above us. I looked up, expecting to see some strange, Jupiterian beast above me, but there was nothing but the writhing limbs and the staring eyes of the great blossoms of the mantrees.

Han Du laughed. "Their nervous systems are of a low order," he said, "and their reactions correspondingly slow and sluggish. It took all this time for the pain of my sword cut to reach the brain of the blossom to which that limb belongs."

"A man's life would never be safe for a moment in such a forest," I commented.

"One has to be constantly on guard," admitted Han Du. "If you ever have to sleep out in the woods, build a smudge. The blossoms don't like smoke. They close up, and then they cannot see to attack you. But be sure that you don't oversleep your smudge."

Vegetable life on Jupiter, practically devoid of sunlight, has developed along entirely different lines from that on earth. Nearly all of it has some animal attributes and nearly all of it is carnivorous, the smaller plants devouring insects, the larger, in turn, depending upon the larger animals for sustenance on up to the maneaters such as I had encountered and those which Han Du said caught and devoured even the hugest animals that exist upon this strange planet.

We posted a couple of guards, who also kept smudges burning; and the rest of us lay down to sleep. One of the men had a chronometer, and this was used to inform the men on guard when to awaken their reliefs. In this way, we all took turns watching and sleeping.

When all had slept, the smudges were allowed to burn more brightly, the men cut limbs from the living trees, sliced them and roasted them. They tasted much like veal. Then we talked over our plans for the future. It was decided that we should split up into parties of two or three and scatter; so that some of us at least might have a chance to escape recapture. They said that the Morgors would hunt us down for a long time. I felt that we would be much safer remaining together as we were ten undefeatable sword-arms; but as the countries from which my companions came were widely scattered; and, as naturally, each wished if possible to return to his own home, it was necessary that we separate.

It chanced that Han Du's country lay in the general direction of Zanor, as did Pho Lar's; so we three bid goodby to the others and left them. How I was to reach faraway Zanor on a planet of twenty-three billion square miles of area, I was at some loss to conceive.

So was Han Du. He told me that I would be welcome in his country—if we were fortunate enough to reach it; but I assured him that I should never cease to search for Zanor and my mate.

NINE

To Zanor!

I SHALL NOT BORE YOU with an account of that part of my odyssey which finally brought me to one of the cities of Han Du's country. We kept as much to cover as we could, since we knew that if Morgors were searching for us, they would be flying low in invisible ships. Forests offered us our best protection from discovery, but there were wide plains to cross, rivers to swim, mountains to climb.

In this world without night, it was difficult to keep account of time; but it seemed to me that we must have traveled for months. Pho Lar remained with us for a great deal of the time, but finally he had to turn away in the direction of his own country. We were sorry to lose him, as he had developed into a splendid companion; and we should miss his sword, too.

We had met no men, but had had several encounters with wild beasts—creatures of hideous, unearthly appearance, both powerful and voracious. I soon realized the inadequacy of our swords as a sole means of defense; so we fashioned spears of a bamboolike growth that seemed wholly vegetable. I also taught Han Du and Pho Lar how to make bows and arrows and to use them. We found them of great advantage in our hunting of smaller animals and birds for food. In the forests, we subsisted almost wholly on the meat of the mantree.

At last Han Du and I came within sight of an ocean. "We are home," he said. "My city lies close beside the sea." I saw no city.

We had come down out of some low hills, and were walking across a narrow coastal plain. Han Du was several yards to my right, when I suddenly bumped into something solid—solid as a brick wall; but there was nothing there! The sudden collision had caused me to step back. I stretched out my hands, and felt what seemed to be a solid wall barring my way, yet only a level expanse of bare ground, but the ground was not entirely bare. It was dotted, here and there, with strange plants—a simple, leafless stock a foot or two tall bearing a single fuzzy blossom at its top.

I looked around for Han Du. He had disappeared! He had just vanished like a punctured soap bubble. All up and down the shore there was no place into which he could have vanished, nothing behind which he would have hidden, no hole in the ground into which he might have darted. I was baffled. I scratched my head in perplexity, as I started on again toward the beach only to once more bump into the wall that was not there.

I put my hands against the invisible wall and followed it. It curved away from me. Foot by foot, I pursued my tantalizing investigation. After a while I was back right where I had started from. It seemed that I had run into an invisible tower of solid air. I started off in a new direction toward the beach, avoiding the obstacle which had obstructed my way. After a dozen paces I ran into another; then I gave up—at least temporarily.

Presently I called Han Du's name aloud, and almost instantly he appeared a short distance from me. "What kind of a game is this?" I demanded. "I bump into a wall of solid air and when I look for you, you are not anywhere, you have disappeared."

Han Du laughed. "I keep forgetting that you are a stranger in this world," he said. "We have come to the city in which I live. I just stepped into my home to greet my family. That is why you could not see me." As he spoke, a woman appeared beside him, and a little child. They seemed to materialize out of thin air. Had I come to a land of disembodied spirits who had the power to materialize? I could scarcely believe it, as there was nothing ghostly nor ethereal about Han Du.

"This is O Ala, my mate," said Han Du. "O Ala, this is John Carter, Prince of Helium. To him we owe my escape from the Morgors."

O Ala extended her hand to me. It was a firm, warm hand of flesh and blood. "Welcome, John Carter," she said. "All that we have is yours."

It was a sweet gesture of hospitality; but as I looked around, I could not see that they had anything. "Where is the city?" I asked.

They both laughed. "Come with us," said O Ala. She led the way, apparently around an invisible corner; and there, before me, I saw an open doorway in thin air. Through the doorway, I could see the interior of a room. "Come in," invited O Ala, and I followed her into a commodious, circular apartment. Han Du followed and closed the door. The roof of the apartment was a dome perhaps twenty feet high at its center. It was divided into four rooms by sliding hangings which could be closed or drawn back against the wall.

"Why couldn't I see the house from the outside?" I asked.

"It is plastered on the outside with sands of invisibility which we find in great quantities along the beach," explained Han Du. "It is about our only protection against the Morgors. Every house in the city is thus protected, a little over five hundred of them."

So I had walked into a city of five hundred houses and seen only an expanse of open beach beside a restless sea. "But where are the people?" I asked. "Are they, too, invisible?"

"Those who are not away, hunting or fishing are in their homes," explained O Ala. "We do not venture out any more than is necessary, lest Morgors be cruising around in their invisible ships and see us; thus discovering our city."

"If any of us should be thus caught out," said Han Du, "he must run away from the city as fast as he can, for if he entered a house, the Morgors would immediately know that there was a city here. It is the sacrifice that each of us is in honor bound to make for the safety of all, for he who runs is almost invariably caught and carried away, unless he chooses to fight and die."

"Tell me," I said to Han Du, "how in the world you found your house, when you could not see it or any other house."

"You noticed the umpalla plants growing throughout the city?" he asked.

"I noticed some plants, but I saw no city."

They both laughed again. "We are so accustomed to it that it does not seem at all strange to us," said O Ala, "but I can understand that it might prove very confusing to a stranger. You see, each plant marks the location of a house. By long experience, each of us has learned the exact location of every house in the city in relation to every other house."

I remained for what may have been five or six days

of earth time in the home of Han Du and O Ala. I met many of their friends, all of whom were gracious and helpful to me in every way that they could be. I was furnished with maps of considerable areas of the planet, parts of which, I was told, were still unexplored even by the Morgors. Of greatest value to me was the fact that Zanor appeared on one of the maps, which also showed that a vast ocean lay between me and the country in which I believed Dejah Thoris to be. How I was to cross this ocean neither I nor my new found friends could offer a suggestion, other than the rather mad scheme I envisioned of building a sail boat and trusting myself to the mad caprices of an unknown sea perhaps swarming with dangerous reptiles. But this I at last decided was the only hope I had for being again reunited with my princess.

There was a forest several miles along the coast from the city, where I might hope to find trees suitable for the construction of my craft. My friends tried their best to dissuade me, but when they found that I was determined to carry out my plan, they loaned me tools; and a dozen of them volunteered to accompany me to the forest and help me build my boat.

At last all was in readiness; and, accompanied by my volunteer helpers, I stepped from the house of Han Du to start the short march to the forest.

Scarcely were we in the open when one of my companions cried, "Morgors!" Whereupon the Savators scattered in all directions away from their city.

"Run, John Carter!" shouted Han Du, but I did not run.

A few yards distant, I saw the open doorway in the side of an invisible ship; and I saw six or seven Morgors emerge from it. Two rushed toward me; the others scattered in pursuit of the Savators. In that instant a new plan flashed across my mind. Hope, almost extinct, leaped to life again.

I whipped my sword from its scabbard and leaped forward to meet the first of the oncoming Morgors, thanking God that there were only two of them, as delay might easily wreck my hopes. There was no finesse in my attack: it was stark, brutal murder; but my conscience did not bother me as I drew my sword from the heart of the first Morgor and faced the second.

The second fellow gave me a little more trouble, as he had been forewarned by the fate of his companion; and, too, he presently recognized me. That made him doubly wary. He commenced to howl to the others, who were pursuing the Savators, to come back and help him, bellowing that here was the creature from Garobus who had led the slaughter at the graduating exercises. From the corner of an eye, I saw that two of them had heard and were returning. I must hurry!

The fellow now fought wholly on the defensive in order to gain time for the others to join him. I had no mind to permit this, and I pressed him hard, often laying myself wide open—a great swordsman could have killed me easily. At last I reached him with a mighty cut that almost severed his head from his body; then, with only a quick glance behind me to see how close the others were, I leaped toward the open doorway of the otherwise invisible ship, a Morgor close upon my heels.

With naked blade still in my hand, I sprang aboard and closed the door behind me; then I wheeled to face whatever of their fellows had been left aboard to guard the craft. The fools had left no one. I had the ship all to myself; and as I ran to the controls I heard the Morgors beating upon the door, angrily demanding that I open it. They must have taken me for a fool, too.

A moment later the ship rose into the air, and I was away upon one of the strangest adventures of my life—navigating an unknown planet in an invisible craft. And I had much to learn about navigation of Jupiter. By watching Vorion, I had learned how to start and stop a Morgor ship, how to gain or lose altitude, and how to cloak the ship in invisibility; but the instruments upon the panel before me were all entirely meaningless to me. The hieroglyphs of the Morgors were quite unintelligible. I had to work it all out for myself.

Opening all the ports, I had a clear field of vision. I could see the shore I had just left, and I knew the direction of the coast line. Han Du had explained this to me. It ran due north and south at that point. The ocean lay to the west of it. I found an instrument which might easily have been a compass; when I altered the course of the ship, I saw that it was a compass. I now had my bearings as closely as it was possible for me to get them. I consulted my map and discovered that Zanor lay almost exactly southeast; so out across that vast expanse of ocean I turned the prow of my ship.

I was free. I had escaped the Morgors unharmed. In Zanor, Dejah Thoris was safe among friends. That I should soon be with her, I had no doubt. We had experienced another amazing adventure. Soon we should be reunited. I had not the slightest doubt of my ability to find Zanor. Perhaps it is because I am always so sure of myself that I so often accomplish the seemingly impossible.

How long I was in crossing that dismal ocean, I do not know. With Jupiter whirling on its axis nearly three times as fast as earth, and with no sun, moon, nor stars, I could not measure time.

I saw no ship upon that entire vast expanse of water, but I did see life—plenty of it. And I saw terrific storms that buffeted my craft, tossing it about like a feather. But that was nothing compared with what I saw below me as the storms at the height of their fury lashed the surface of the waters. I realized then how suicidal would have been my attempt to cross that terrible ocean in the frail craft that I had planned to build. I saw waves that must have measured two hundred feet from trough to crest—waves that hurled the mighty monsters of the deep as though they had been tiny minnows. No ship could have lived in such seas. I realized then why I saw no shipping on this great Jupiterian ocean.

But at last I sighted land ahead—and what land! Zan Dar had told me of the mighty mountains of Zanor rearing their forested heads twenty miles above the level of the sea, and it was such mountains that lay ahead of me. If I had reckoned accurately, this should be Zanor; and these breath-taking mountains assured me that I had not gone wrong.

I knew from Zan Dar's explanation, just where to search for the stamping grounds of his tribe—a wild mountain and at an altitude of only about ten miles, or meadows and ravines on the east slope of the highest mountain and at an altitude of only about ten miles, or about halfway to the summit. Here the air is only slightly thinner than at sea level, as the cloud envelope retains the atmosphere of Jupiter as though it were held in a bag, permitting none of it to escape, while the rapid revolution of the planet tends to throw the atmosphere far up from the surface.

Most fortunate was I in coming upon the village of Zan Dar with little or no difficulty. Entirely invisible, I hovered above it, dropping down slowly. I knew that the moment they saw a Morgor ship, they would disappear into the forests that surrounded the village, waiting there to rush upon any Morgors who might be foolish enough to leave the ship after landing.

There were people in plain view of me in the village as I dropped to within fifty feet of the ground. I stopped the ship and hung there, then I demagnetized the hull; and, as the ship became instantly visible, I leaped to the door and pushed it open; so that they could see that I was no Morgor. I waved to them and shouted that I was a friend of Zan Dar, and asked permission to land.

They called to me to do so, and I brought the ship slowly toward the ground. My lonely voyage was over. I had surmounted seemingly unsurmountable obstacles and I had reached my goal. Soon my incomparable Dejah Thoris would be again in my arms.

ABOUT EDGAR RICE BURROUGHS

EDGAR RICE BURROUGHS is one of the world's most popular authors. With no previous experience as an author, he wrote and sold his first novel—*A Princess of Mars*—in 1912. In the ensuing thirty-eight years until his death in 1950, Burroughs wrote 91 books and a host of short stories and articles. Although best known as the creator of the classic *Tarzan of the Apes* and *John Carter of Mars,* his restless imagination knew few bounds. Burroughs' prolific pen ranged from the American West to primitive Africa and on to romantic adventure on the moon, the planets, and even beyond the farthest star.

No one knows how many copies of ERB books have been published throughout the world. It is conservative to say, however, that of the translations into 32 known languages, including Braille, the number must run into the hundreds of millions. When one considers the additional world-wide following of the Tarzan newspaper feature, radio programs, comic magazines, motion pictures and television, Burroughs must have been known and loved by literally a thousand million or more.